— YOUNG READERS' EDITION —

THREE DAYS

—— IN ——

JANUARY

DWIGHT EISENHOWER'S
FINAL MISSION

— YOUNG READERS' EDITION —

THREE DAYS
— IN —
JANUARY

DWIGHT EISENHOWER'S
FINAL MISSION

BRET BAIER

WITH CATHERINE WHITNEY

HARPER

An Imprint of HarperCollinsPublishers

Library of Congress Control Number: 2019944615
ISBN 978-0-06-291534-4

Typography by Catherine San Juan
19 20 21 22 23   PC/LSCH   10 9 8 7 6 5 4 3 2 1

First Edition

To our sons, Paul and Daniel, and their generation.
Please allow history to inform your decisions in the future.

— CONTENTS —

— A PERSONAL MESSAGE —
FROM BRET BAIER

I am very happy to bring you this book about President Dwight D. Eisenhower and his lasting importance to the life of the United States. As you read the inside story of his wisdom and heroism and learn about the significance of his final three days in office, I hope you see that it is not just an abstract tale of the past. History is a living thing, and we can find insight and inspiration from the leaders of previous eras.

Studying Eisenhower's life was a very rewarding experience for me. I was not alive during his presidency, but my interest in him developed over the years, especially after I visited the famous golf course in Augusta, Georgia, where Ike had a mini White House. It was filled with fascinating memorabilia, and I began to get very interested in this president I knew so little about.

I'm the Fox News chief political anchor and host of *Special Report with Bret Baier*. As a journalist, I'm naturally curious, and once I get interested in a topic I can't let it go. So I traveled to Abilene, Kansas, to visit the Eisenhower Presidential Library, Museum and Boyhood Home. It is a beautiful and even majestic setting, surrounded by fields of grain and alive with Eisenhower's historic contributions—from his commanding role in the Allied victory over Hitler to his decisive management of Cold War threats during the Soviet rise. The library and museum are built on the site of Ike's childhood home, which sits fully intact on its original lot—a typical modest turn-of-the-century house where you could pile in six or seven boys, with beds squeezed into every corner, while still leaving space for a piano.

The archivists at the library told me that if I wanted to learn more about Eisenhower, there were millions of pages of documents and hundreds of thousands of feet of original film—some of it still unread and unseen. There was even a locked vault containing thousands of pages of material still classified after all these years. Now my reporter's curiosity was *really* piqued. Although the library hosts some 200,000 visitors a year, coming from across America and around the world, most Americans will never physically visit the heartland site. I wanted to bring it to them.

Being at the presidential library has a strange effect. You start to feel as if you're standing in that time gone by. I work in television, which is a visual medium, so I could easily picture the scenes—the barefoot boy; the general, head in hands, preparing to make the critical decision about D-Day; the grinning candidate America *liked* (the slogan of his first presidential campaign was

"I Like Ike"); the living room president, who spoke regularly on the small screen, glasses slipping down his nose; the confident commander in chief, standing toe to toe with Khrushchev. In particular, I could imagine the purposeful elder, preparing for his final mission in January 1961—those crucial days that are the centerpiece of this book.

As I dug through the files, combed through the oral histories, listened to the tapes, and read the books about Eisenhower's presidency, one reality stood out for me: here was a man on a mission to save America, who largely succeeded in that endeavor. His was not the dramatic leadership of an era with bombs bursting in midair, but the wise course of a military strategist who rescued the world from that inevitability. He was a leader, in the truest sense of the word, and from my perch in the twenty-first century I was drawn to the question of what made him great.

The historian Jon Meacham made an observation that hit the mark. Referring to FDR and Churchill in Ken Burns's documentary series *The Roosevelts*, he said, "One of the mysteries of history is why is it that certain moments produce exactly the right human beings?" I came to see that Eisenhower, our thirty-fourth president, was such a man. He was the buried treasure of the past century—his influence underappreciated in the clamor of great individuals jockeying for recognition.

And it's all there to be found at the Eisenhower Library. I hope you get a chance to visit it one day, along with other presidential libraries, which tell our nation's story in a vivid way.

I invite you to read this book and feel the pull of history. Imagine being there. Think about how you—and we as a country—can use the lessons of Ike's leadership in the present. Most of all, enjoy the read, and let history come alive for you.

Bret Baier

December 2019

Introduction:

THE FINAL MISSION

DWIGHT "IKE" EISENHOWER, THE thirty-fourth president of the United States, was exactly the right man for his moment in history. Despite his role as an American hero, his influence and importance remain largely unappreciated. We easily speak of men like Franklin Roosevelt, who led us through a great world war, or Ronald Reagan, who faced off with Soviet leader Mikhail Gorbachev to help wind down the Cold War. But many of us overlook the man whose epic presidency saved the world from nuclear disaster and challenged Americans to consider how to use the nation's power for the greater good. These themes were the centerpiece of Ike's farewell address, delivered on January 17, 1961, three days before John F. Kennedy became president.

The contrast between Eisenhower and Kennedy was striking. Ike was born in the nineteenth century and was sixty-two years old when he entered the White House. Kennedy, on the other hand, was just forty-four years old, making him the youngest person ever elected president. By 1960, the American people had grown weary of the world they knew, and they were captivated by the idea of a different path. Ike represented the sleepy 1950s; Kennedy held the promise of the future. The tan, movie-star-handsome president, with his gorgeous wife, Jackie, and two adorable children came to symbolize the American family we wanted to be. The Kennedys embodied the way America wanted to see itself—young, worldly, smart, and educated.

The truth was more complex. For starters, the 1950s weren't so sleepy after all. Eisenhower took office at one of the most dangerous times in American history. The world was struggling to reorder itself after World War II. The Soviet Union and China were expanding their communist influence, and the Korean conflict remained unsettled. The choices Eisenhower made in those crucial years may have saved the world from nuclear war.

On the other hand, Kennedy's New Frontier would prove to be rocky territory—something Ike predicted. His warning, delivered in personal meetings with

Kennedy and in his farewell address to the nation, was his final mission, an effort to draw a road map for the future and protect the investment he had made in peace. *Three Days in January* goes behind the scenes to detail those final days, in the process taking a measure of the man who made such a difference to the life of the nation.

In his meetings with Kennedy and his farewell address to the nation, President Eisenhower was concerned about the future. He asked the question—still an essential question today—How should America use its military might in the world?

Eisenhower was a military man who never shied away from the necessary use of force, but he knew the cost of war. Ike was clear-eyed about the devastating potential of nuclear weapons. Never before or since has any president been as confident in his understanding of the role of the military in a nation's identity. Eisenhower believed it was critical that the United States use its exceptional position in the world not to wage war but to create a lasting peace.

Part 1

THE SETTING

1

THE FIRST VISIT
DECEMBER 6, 1960
9:00 A.M.
THE WHITE HOUSE

PRESIDENT-ELECT JOHN F. KENNEDY arrived at the White House alone. He stepped out of his car to the flash of press cameras and a chorus of "The Stars and Stripes Forever" by the U.S. Marine Band. Members of the army, navy, air force, and marines lined the driveway to salute him. President Dwight Eisenhower had ordered the grand reception, hoping to welcome and impress the new president-elect.

Eisenhower hadn't enjoyed that kind of welcome when he took over the presidency from Harry S. Truman in 1953. Truman and Eisenhower had once been close, and in many ways were alike, having grown up only 150 miles from each other. However, harsh rhetoric from the campaign had destroyed any civility between them. "The general doesn't know any more about politics than a pig knows about Sunday," Truman said, even though at one time he had urged Eisenhower to run for president. He was disappointed that Ike, who had previously kept his party affiliation private, had decided to run as a Republican, and then had criticized Truman during the campaign.

The single meeting between the two men after the election was brief and chilly, lasting only twenty minutes and offering little substance. Clearly, Truman didn't trust Ike, and the feeling was mutual. When thinking about appearing with Truman during the inauguration, Eisenhower said, "I wonder if I can stand sitting next to him." As a matter of tradition, the president and president-elect would meet at the White House for a preinauguration cup of coffee. On Ike's inauguration day, the Eisenhowers refused to join the Trumans before the ceremony. Instead, they chose to wait in the car that would take the president and president-elect to the ceremony.

Now that Eisenhower was preparing to leave the White House, he was determined to do things differently. He wanted to orchestrate a smooth transition.

The respect Ike showed Kennedy was a hopeful bet on the future. Eisenhower wanted to see Kennedy succeed. He understood that his legacy was made not just by the actions of his administration while he was in office, but also by the way history unfolded after the torch was passed.

Although Kennedy had served in the U.S. Senate during Eisenhower's eight years in office, the two men didn't know each other well. Most of Eisenhower's impressions of Kennedy had been formed during the 1960 campaign, when Kennedy ran against Vice President Richard Nixon. Eisenhower was depressed by Nixon's loss, considering it the biggest defeat of his own political life.

Ike felt guilty that he had not campaigned harder for Nixon. He had tried to respect his vice president's wishes, and Nixon wanted to keep Ike out of the election, preferring to run as his own man. He didn't want to be seen as "Ike's boy." In hindsight, it is clear that Nixon underestimated the challenge Kennedy presented.

While overconfidence surely played a role in Nixon's decision to sideline the president, Ike also had a nagging feeling that Nixon didn't fully trust him. Their relationship had been tarnished by an incident that occurred at the end of his first term. As Ike was planning his campaign for reelection, he called Nixon into the Oval

Office. The president said he wasn't sure that the vice presidency was the best platform from which to start a presidential campaign. He offered Nixon a chance to switch to a cabinet post.

Nixon was shocked—and suspicious. Was Eisenhower trying to dump him from the ticket?

The president tried to reassure Nixon that he had confidence in him, but it was too late. The damage to their relationship had already been done. Nixon decided to stick with the vice presidency, but Ike felt that Nixon never fully got over his suspicions. When 1960 rolled around, Nixon kept Eisenhower on the sidelines, even though the president was popular and may have helped bring in votes. When Ike warned Nixon not to do a televised debate with Kennedy, Nixon wouldn't listen. The debate proved to be a disaster. In fact, it was so devastating for Nixon that JFK's mother, Rose Kennedy, said she felt sorry for Nixon's mother and wondered if she should call her to offer condolences.

When Eisenhower campaigned for Nixon in the last week of the campaign, he was disheartened to see signs that read "We Like Ike But We Back Jack."

Once Kennedy won the election, Ike wasn't interested in holding on to personal resentments. He understood that the language of a campaign could be insulting. If Ike was offended by the characterization of Kennedy as a fresh example of the "New Frontier" and of himself as an out-of-date relic of the past, he didn't say anything about it.

Eisenhower was more concerned with whether Kennedy's campaign rhetoric represented his true beliefs. In particular, Ike worried about Kennedy's reckless charge that the Soviet Union was producing more nuclear missiles than the United States. "We are facing a gap on which we are gambling with our survival," said Kennedy. Eisenhower worried that Kennedy might believe his own propaganda. In truth, if there was a missile gap, it was in favor of the United States.

The president felt Kennedy had won the election by portraying the Eisenhower administration as weak in the face of the Soviet threat. As he prepared to meet with Kennedy, Ike felt a sense of urgency to communicate the exact nature of the threat they faced. Now that they were meeting face-to-face, Ike was intent on taking the true measure of the man. What kind of president would he be, and what could Ike say that would help guide him on the right course?

IKE SCHOOLS KENNEDY

Kennedy bounded up the portico steps and firmly shook Ike's hand. "Mr. President, it's good to be here," Kennedy said. They went to the Oval Office for a private conversation. From the moment they sat across from each other, both men were at ease.

Kennedy seemed sincere and respectful once the full seriousness of the moment struck him. He wanted to hear what Ike had to say. Ike was pleased to find the younger man's attitude to be that of a "serious, earnest seeker for information."

Kennedy was very interested in the White House—the administrative organization, the cabinet, and the national security establishment. However, as Ike detailed his national security process, he noticed that Kennedy seemed dismissive. Kennedy seemed to regard the decision-making process as more informal. Ike tried to impress on him how much he needed to use a well-organized security team. The president urged Kennedy to leave the system in place for a time, at least until he was intimately familiar with the problems facing the country.

The two men discussed the most pressing foreign policy issues of the day, including the fighting in Vietnam and Southeast Asia, where 600 American advisors were stationed. The president also faced a looming problem in Berlin, which had been divided between democratic West Berlin and Soviet-controlled communist East Berlin. Ike had avoided a showdown with the Soviets over the city, but tensions ran high. On the matter of Cuba, Kennedy had already been briefed on a plan under way to train Cuban exiles for a mission designed to lead to the overthrow of Fidel Castro's regime. Kennedy favored the plan, although Ike cautioned him that it was very much in the early stages.

Eisenhower addressed the issue of missiles head-on, describing the administration's efforts to work through NATO—the North Atlantic Treaty Organization—to form an alliance that would strengthen both the United States and its allies.

Kennedy asked if Eisenhower thought he should plan a personal visit with Soviet premier Nikita Khrushchev early in his term. Ike recommended he wait until his presidency was more firmly established. Eisenhower warned that Khrushchev was sly; he had an agenda. More to the point, the Soviet leader was answerable to the Politburo, the policymaking committee of the Communist Party, so his policies and actions were shaped by hard-liners who wanted to outsmart the Americans. It would be a tough meeting.

After their private discussion, Eisenhower and Kennedy went to the Cabinet Room, where the secretaries of state, defense, and treasury were prepared for a briefing. Also present were Kennedy's advisor Clark Clifford and Eisenhower's chief of staff Wilton Persons. Ike emphasized the importance of the cabinet, which he used as a high-level study group. He knew it was crucial to get the most and best out of people, so Ike employed a style of leadership that was not top-down. Ike's military experience taught him to build up the members of the team so that they could shine. He understood that leadership was about more than dominating a room.

Ike believed the times demanded thoughtful leadership, a steady hand on the tiller. The only way to win World War III was to prevent it. He knew that military arms were not a guarantee of peace and security. Under Ike's watch, the nuclear arsenal had grown substantially, but he viewed these weapons as a costly insurance policy for a catastrophe that must be prevented.

As Eisenhower ushered Kennedy out of the White House after three hours and forty minutes, warmly taking his arm, Kennedy asked if he might call on Eisenhower in the future if he needed advice. Of course, Ike said, with an easy grin, reminding Kennedy to consider his age and his well-earned retirement.

In reality, Ike wasn't thinking about retirement. As he walked back to his office, his heart was pumping. He had six weeks to make his final move. Ike intended to close out his presidency with a world-changing message. Rather than going meekly into the night, Eisenhower believed that he could set a course for the fate of the civilized world and his beloved country. His plan would come to fruition over three critical days in January 1961.

BECOMING IKE

IT IS A STRIKING fact that Dwight Eisenhower—the nation's most famous soldier—was born to parents whose religion opposed all wars. While his parents were very important to him, there were a number of other forces that shaped the behavior and outlook of the thirty-fourth president.

As a young man, Eisenhower didn't consider himself an exceptional student or a particularly promising military candidate. He once told his wife, Mamie, "If I'm lucky, I'll be a colonel." Yet he went on to become a five-star general and the supreme allied commander—the head of the Allied forces during World War II—and he assembled the greatest fighting force in the history of mankind. Under his leadership, the Allied forces defeated Adolf Hitler's war machine and saved Western civilization from fascism. Ike never dreamed of being a general, much less president of the United States, but that's where life took him.

When he was a boy, Ike was taught to be honest, humble, and hardworking. He grew up in a community grounded in faith and hard work. His exceptional intuition, strategic intellect, and warm personality were part nature and part nurture. He had the ability to inspire and elevate those who worked under his leadership.

Dwight David Eisenhower—who became "little Ike" and then "Ike" in childhood—was born in Denison, Texas, on October 14, 1890. He was the third of seven brothers, one of whom died as an infant. His parents, David and Ida Stover Eisenhower, met while students at Lane University in Lecompton, Kansas, a religious school run by the Church of the United Brethren in Christ. Ida dropped out of school to marry, but her life-long love of learning was passed on to her sons.

As newlyweds, David and Ida received a gift of farmland from David's parents, but David didn't want to be a farmer. Instead, he mortgaged the land to his brother-in-law and opened a retail store in Hope, Kansas. The business failed, and David took a job with the railroad in Denison. Ike and his brother Roy were born there before the family returned to Kansas, settling in Abilene, where Ike's father worked as a mechanical engineer at the Belle Springs Creamery. Ike thought of Abilene as home. It is the site of his presidential library and burial plot.

When Ike was five, his parents joined the Jehovah's Witnesses following the death of their son Paul. The religion taught that death was only a state of sleeping and promised that they would be reunited with their son soon. The Eisenhowers' religion isn't always clearly identified in historical writings. Ike avoided talking about his parents' faith, perhaps because it was unconventional or because it opposed not only war but also politics and government.

Ike was uncomfortable with organized religion as an adult, but his underlying faith was ever present. During Eisenhower's administration "under God" was added to the Pledge of Allegiance, and he signed the law making "In God We Trust" the national motto. He initiated the National Prayer Breakfast and the National Day of Prayer. He was baptized only after being elected president, joining the National Presbyterian Church in Washington, DC.

Eisenhower's small-town roots also had an influence on him. Abilene in the late 1800s was known primarily as the end of the road, the final destination for cattle drives moving north from Texas on the Chisholm Trail.

Ike spoke about his hometown in a speech in 1953: "I was raised in a little town of which most of you have never heard, but in the West it is a famous place. It is called Abilene, Kansas . . . Now that town had a code, and I was raised as a boy to prize that code. It was: meet anyone face-to-face with whom you disagree." Ike followed this code of conduct all his life. It was one reason he despised politics. He hated underhandedness and fakery; his leadership style was based on frankness and an effort to be authentic and live up to the motto "what you see is what you get."

The Eisenhower homestead on Fourth Street, purchased in 1898 when Ike was eight for $3,500, was literally on the wrong side of the tracks, with the train tracks running both in front of and behind the house. The hissing sound of the steam engine and the clanging of the bell were the audible backdrop to Ike's childhood. The house was humble, but included a large orchard, a robust vegetable garden, and an alfalfa field. There were chickens, a cow, and a horse. When the chores were divvied up among the six boys, their least favorite was working inside the house, with so much going on outdoors. And the best chore of all—which all of the brothers vied for—was being allowed to go to the store and bring the groceries home. What attracted the boys was a "dill pickle jar that you could dive into, sometimes arm deep almost, and try to get one," making the trip worthwhile.

"In retrospect," Ike once said, "I realize that we might have been classified as being poor, but we didn't know it." He added that this willful ignorance was part of the glory of America. "All that we knew was that our parents—of great courage—could say to us, 'Opportunity is all about you. Reach out and take it.'"

Ike admitted he was something of a scamp as a kid, and he had a temper. He often told the story of an incident that occurred on Halloween night when he was ten. His older brothers were allowed to go trick-or-treating, but his parents thought Ike was too young to go. He was furious with their decision, and he responded by running into the yard and smashing his fists into the trunk of an apple tree until they bled. His father dragged him back into the house and sent him to bed, where he lay sobbing, full of humiliation, disappointment, and frustration. About an hour later, Ike's mother came in and sat beside him. As she ministered to his bleeding hands, she told him that mastering his temper was the task of growing up. She quoted the Bible, saying, "He that conquereth his own soul is greater than he who taketh a city."

Ike tried to live up to his mother's words. As an adult, he became well known for his calm strength under pressure. He developed a simple method for handling rage, an "anger drawer" in his desk into which he dropped slips of paper with the names of people he was angry at. Once the paper was in the drawer, he let go of his complaint and didn't think about it anymore.

WEST POINT–BOUND

In his childhood, Ike spent much of his free time reading. He devoured histories, sometimes to the point where he neglected his homework and chores. The worst punishment his mother could give him was to take away his books, which she sometimes did when Ike became too distracted. His mother put the books in a cabinet under lock and key. One day Ike found the key. Whenever his mother went shopping or outside to work in the vegetable garden, he would open the cabinet and reclaim his precious books.

Eisenhower was also passionate about sports, baseball and football in particular. An accident during his freshman year of high school threatened his athletic career. One day, when running with friends, Ike stumbled and fell, scraping his knee. He didn't think much of it at first, but two days later, he was feverish and delirious with infection. Antibiotics had not yet been discovered, and Ike slipped in and out of consciousness. When he heard the doctor use the word *amputation*, Ike snapped awake.

He told his brother Edgar, "I'd rather be dead than crippled and not be able to play ball."

Ike's parents supported their son's decision to refuse the amputation, even though his condition grew more desperate. Eventually he recovered, but Ike missed school for the rest of the year. As a result of his illness, Ike graduated from high school behind his peers. He wasn't sure what to do next. After high school, with no money for college, Ike worked at the creamery. A close friend of his attended a private military high school and suggested that Ike request an appointment to a military academy so that he could receive a free education and a chance to play sports. Ike was afraid he would never be able to afford college on his own.

On August 20, 1910, Ike sent a letter to Kansas U.S. senator Joseph Bristow. "Dear Sir," he wrote, "I would very much like to enter either the school at Annapolis, or the one at West Point. In order to do this, I must have an appointment to one of these places, and so I am writing to you in order to secure the same . . . If you find it possible to appoint me to one of these schools, your kindness will certainly be appreciated by me."

Attached to his letter were letters of support from influential men in Abilene, who praised the family and vouched for Ike's character.

Ike was rejected by the U.S. Naval Academy, in

Annapolis, Maryland, because he was older than the admission age, but he scored second place on the qualification exam for West Point. A short time later, he moved into the first-place slot after the other candidate failed the height requirement. A second entrance exam sealed his acceptance, and he was told to report to the U.S. Military Academy at West Point on June 14, 1911.

Ike's parents hated war and might have been troubled by their son's choice of West Point, but they never showed their feelings. They believed that Ike had the right to live his life as he saw fit. Ike's brother Milton, who was twelve at the time, remembered the day Ike left for West Point: "Dad was at work when Ike left. I went out on the west porch with mother as Ike started uptown, carrying his suitcase, to take the train. Mother stood there like a statue, and I stood right by her until Ike was out of sight. Then she came in and went to her room and bawled like a baby."

In his early weeks at West Point, Ike spent his recreation periods on the baseball field. The coach told Ike he was impressed with his fielding but didn't think much of his hitting style. "Practice hitting my way for a year, and you'll be on my squad next spring," the coach said. But Ike was too impatient. He tried out for football and made the team as a linebacker. Perhaps the highlight of his football career was a 1912 game between West Point and the famed Carlisle Indians, whose star player, Jim Thorpe, had just won Olympic gold medals in the pentathlon and the decathlon at the Stockholm Games. The Indians won, and soon after Ike suffered a knee injury that ended his football days.

Ike's class at West Point—the class of 1915—would come to be known as "the class the stars fell upon" because of the number of graduates who went on to become generals: two five-star generals (Ike and Omar Bradley), two four-star generals, seven three-star lieutenant generals, twenty-four two-star major generals, and twenty-four one-star brigadier generals.

Ike, who reached the top of military success, was a somewhat unimpressive student, with frequent discipline problems. It's not that he lacked intellect, but he downplayed his smarts to be one of the guys, a quality that would win him praise and scorn throughout his life. He despised pretentiousness, so he was often underestimated. As he approached graduation in 1915, there was a question about whether he'd receive a commission. Out of 164 graduates, Eisenhower ranked 61st academically and 125th in discipline. He got into trouble frequently, but most of the issues were fairly minor. His disciplinary infractions included dancing (a repeated offense), lateness, and sloppiness, among others.

At age twenty-five, Eisenhower was assigned as a

second lieutenant to Fort Sam Houston in San Antonio, Texas, for the pay of $141.67 a month. He arrived at his post on September 13, 1915, tasked with training the enlisted men. War had been raging in Europe for more than a year, and many people, including Ike, believed that America would eventually join the war effort.

In San Antonio he met the woman who would become his wife. Eighteen-year-old Mamie Doud from Denver was spending the winter in San Antonio with her wealthy parents when she met Ike. He asked if she'd like to accompany him on his rounds, and she said yes. They began dating and became engaged on Valentine's Day. Mamie was in love, but she was young and had lived a pampered life. Her father was extremely protective of her, and he only agreed to the engagement if they waited to marry until the end of the year. He also exerted some control over Ike's choice of specialty.

At the time, Ike wanted to join the Aviation Section and become a pilot. He was accepted, but Mamie's father told him he would not support the wedding if Ike became a pilot. Flying itself was only a decade old, and fighter pilots from the Royal Flying Corps had an average survival period of eleven days. Love ultimately won out, and Ike announced that he would not join the Aviation Section. Ike and Mamie were married in Denver on July 1, 1916.

When the United States finally declared war on Germany and joined the war on April 6, 1917, Ike longed to head overseas to lead a platoon. Instead he was kept at home, training other soldiers to fight.

During the war years, Mamie became pregnant and gave birth to their son, Doud Dwight, whom they nicknamed "Icky." Three years later, Icky contracted scarlet fever; he died on January 2, 1921. Ike called it "a tragedy from which we never recovered." Throughout his life, he regularly expressed his deep grief over the loss, as if it were still fresh, even many decades later. Every year on Icky's birthday, Ike sent Mamie yellow roses, which he claimed were Icky's favorite.

Ike was dazed and depressed during the months after his son's death. Ambition seemed pointless. It was with some surprise that he learned that the army approved his transfer to Panama, where Ike would serve under Major General Fox Conner. The general proved to be just the father figure and mentor Ike needed during this difficult time in his life. Conner had an extensive knowledge of military history and often asked Ike to consider what *he* would do if faced with circumstances similar to those in history. This practice helped Ike develop a keen sense of military strategy.

Within a year, Mamie was pregnant again. She flew home to Denver in the final months of her pregnancy;

Ike joined her there to see his son John Sheldon Doud Eisenhower born on August 3, 1922. John would be the couple's only living child.

PREPARING TO LEAD

After two years in Panama, Ike began a series of postings that appeared to be grooming him for future promotions. The young family moved from Colorado to Kansas to Washington, DC. In 1933, Ike received an assignment that marked a shift in his career. He was assigned to work for General Douglas MacArthur, the army's chief of staff.

At first Ike felt sidelined, but he recognized the opportunity presented by working for General MacArthur. Eisenhower had never known someone as forceful, personable, and demanding, with a brilliant, encyclopedic knowledge of the military, politics, and history. In 1935, Ike had the chance to plan the defense program for the newly established Philippine Commonwealth. Although MacArthur was in charge, Ike had a great deal of responsibility. Ike was the man on the scene for long hours each day, and he began to take on the manner of a commander.

MacArthur noted Eisenhower's leadership skills. "This is the best officer in the army," MacArthur wrote about Ike. "When the next war comes, he should go right to the top."

The two men had different leadership styles. Mac-Arthur was authoritarian and often wielded power in an arrogant and brutal manner. Ike was a listener; he wanted to study and reflect on a situation after hearing what other people had to say. "You do not lead by hitting people over the head," he said. "That's assault, not leadership." Eisenhower favored conversations based on mutual respect; he considered leadership "the art of getting someone else to do something you want done because he wants to do it."

Ike's leadership skills were put to the test as the world entered another war. On September 1, 1939, Hitler invaded Poland, and Britain and France declared war on Germany. The United States was not yet engaged in the war, but the War Department wanted Ike back home as an instructor for enlisted men. He was assigned to Fort Lewis, in Washington State, as chief of staff of the Third Army. He was at that posting for less than a year before being assigned to Fort Sam Houston—the place his military career had begun—in the same role.

Ike and Mamie arrived in San Antonio in the summer of 1941. Their son John was at West Point, and Ike and Mamie worried about him becoming a cadet with the world at war. On December 7, 1941, Ike was napping when Mamie heard the news of the Japanese attack on Pearl Harbor over the radio. She quickly woke him, and five days later he received a message from Washington, at the request of Army Chief of Staff General George C. Marshall: "The chief says for you to hop a plane and get up here right away."

Marshall could not have been more different from MacArthur. Marshall did not tolerate pessimists or people interested in self-promotion. He was formal, one of the rare people who didn't use Ike's nickname. Initially, Marshall sought out Ike for his experience in the Philippines. He had been impressed by Ike's plan to defend the Philippines, which had been invaded by the Japanese only hours after Pearl Harbor. Ike seemed to have a special ability to develop complex strategic plans.

Eisenhower designed a plan for a unified assault by the Allied powers (the United States, Britain, France, the Soviet Union, and Australia, among other countries) against the Axis powers (Germany, Italy, and Japan, among other countries). In particular, he focused on an assault in North Africa, which would serve as a beachhead in the war effort.

On June 8, 1942, Ike presented a draft of his report, "Directive for the Commanding General European Theater of Operations," presenting a plan for a unified command of the Allied forces. Ike mentioned to Marshall that this was one document he should read carefully, because it could serve as a blueprint for the course of the war.

"I certainly do want to read it," Marshall said. "You may be the man who executes it. If that's the case, when can you leave?"

That was Ike's first hint that he might be headed overseas. Three days later—after more than twenty-five years in the army—he was going to war for the first time. He traveled to West Point and took his son John out for a boat ride, where he broke the news that he was leaving for England.

"What's your job going to be over there?" John asked.

"Well, I'm going to be the boss."

John asked him what that meant.

"I'm going to be the commanding general," he replied.

"My God!" John exclaimed, realizing the importance of his father's role. Not only was he going to war, he was going to be the man leading the charge.

3

IKE IN COMMAND

ON JUNE 24, 1942, General Dwight Eisenhower flew to London to take command of the operation he had planned in North Africa. There wasn't a moment to lose. His plan was to open up a pathway from North Africa to Sicily, to mainland Italy, and into Europe. This would allow the Allies a way to get troops into the heart of Europe to fight the Nazis.

The chief threat to the mission was that the region was under control of Vichy France, French forces that were sympathetic to Hitler. The success of the campaign depended on the French forces not putting up too much opposition to the Allies.

Ike built a unified fighting force. He made it clear he

would not tolerate any dissent between the British and American soldiers. "We are in this together as Allies," Eisenhower said. "We will fight it shoulder to shoulder. Men will be praised or blamed for what they do, not for their nationality."

The operation was coordinated from Gibraltar, a British beachhead in Spain that was the ideal spot to monitor the ships at sea. Inside the Rock of Gibraltar was a virtual city of tunnels, rooms, and working areas. Among these dark and gloomy passages, Eisenhower set up his command center on November 5, three days before the invasion.

Even though the conditions were desolate and unpleasant, Ike understood that strong leadership involved portraying an attitude of optimism and confidence in victory. He tried to remain positive.

Three landings, at Casablanca, Oran, and Algiers, were planned for 1 a.m. on November 8. As massive convoys of warships and cargo ships made their way to the area from England, Ireland, and America, Ike waited for news of the landings. In the tomb-like catacombs of his Gibraltar headquarters, Ike had no way of knowing the full extent of the German response—whether the Allied ships passing through the narrow Strait of Gibraltar would be bombarded, sunk, or set aflame at sea, spilling thousands of men into the deep, cold waters of the strait. Also unknown was whether the Vichy French forces would mount a fight against the Allies.

As it turned out, all three landings were successful, with little Vichy French resistance and few Allied casualties. With a foothold in North Africa, the Allies began off-loading troops, transports, and supplies, pushing across North Africa and eventually into Italy. This early success gave Eisenhower hope that the Nazis could be defeated and the war could be won.

IKE PLANS D-DAY

Having succeeded in the first line of attack, Eisenhower began to plan the most critical maneuver of all—a direct invasion of France known as Operation Overlord. In December 1943, Ike received word that President Roosevelt wanted to meet with him. When they met, the president got straight to the point: "Well, Ike," he said, "you are going to command Overlord."

Ike was surprised by the assignment. The obvious choice for such a role was General Marshall, but Roosevelt needed him as an advisor in Washington.

"Mr. President, I realize that such an appointment involved difficult decisions," Ike said. "I hope you will not be disappointed."

Of course, the decision to appoint Ike had not been made lightly. It was based on the very different personalities of all the major officers capable of such a command. And Ike's masterful work with the invasion of North Africa was taken into consideration. Although Ike thought the title "supreme commander" was boastful, he was pleased to have the job.

The war effort was a study in male ego. For the Allies, the leading figures were British prime minister Winston Churchill, leader of the French Resistance Charles de Gaulle, American president Franklin Delano Roosevelt, and King George VI, who often wished he were not king of the United Kingdom so he could join the fight. These leaders were supported by imposing military giants, such as American generals Omar Bradley and George Patton, and British general Bernard Montgomery. It could have been a disaster of clashing egos were it not for the mutual decision to stand behind the leadership of General Eisenhower.

It was Ike's responsibility to form a unified strategy and to keep the various personalities under control. He had a confident presence that made him seem larger than his height of five ten and a half inches. He did not celebrate war. He was not a bull charging into battle, but a strategist whose field was the map room and the conference table. Ike compared his role as supreme commander to chairman of the board—responsible, yet a hair removed from the daily tasks.

"He's not the greatest soldier in the world," said Montgomery. "His real strength lies in his human qualities.

He has the power of drawing the hearts of men toward him."

But it wasn't just his personality. Ike also had a talent for seeing the big picture. With Nazi Germany in control of most of Western Europe, a daring plan was necessary to shake loose the Nazi grip.

Operation Overlord—also known as D-Day—was a staggering enterprise. The Allied planners knew that there would be enormous Allied casualties, but they had to move forward anyway. Without success on D-Day, the war might have been lost.

The scale of the invasion was hard to imagine: 5,000 sea vessels, 13,000 aircraft, and more than 160,000 men prepared to sweep down on the beaches of Normandy. More than 16,000 staff were involved in the planning. At Ike's insistence, this was a far larger force than had originally been planned for. He felt strongly that an overwhelming force was the key to success. It all had to be done in secret because the element of surprise was crucial. The invasion was scheduled for June 5, 1944, a night when the moon would be full to provide some light and the tides would be low enough to support a landing.

Eisenhower worried about the inevitable loss of life. He made a point to visit the troops whenever possible. In the months leading up to D-Day he personally visited twenty-six divisions, twenty-four airfields, five ships of war, and many other installations. He wanted to check on preparations and to lift morale. "Soldiers like to see the men who are directing operations," Ike later wrote.

At Southwick House, the invasion headquarters in the southern English town of Portsmouth, Ike and the core group of invasion strategists studied the plans, looking for any flaws. The mission was orchestrated like a ballet, a detailed dance in which each new wave of soldiers entered into the battle at its precisely designated time. Paratroopers would drop from the skies in the dark early hours of June 6; air assaults would begin on the surrounding bridges; transport planes would drop men and supplies along the beaches; and at dawn, troops would begin landing on the beaches.

It was a well-designed plan. But as the saying goes, "Man plans, God laughs." The most important issue became the weather.

Weather on the English Channel was unpredictable in the best of times, and a stormy forecast could make the invasion impossible. It was very bad news on June 4 when the chief meteorologist of Operation Overlord told Ike that he expected a storm to roll in across the channel. He urged Ike to delay the invasion by a day.

Would one day be enough? Meteorologists in 1944 had none of the sophisticated equipment used today to predict the weather. How long could they wait? If they waited two weeks for another window in the tides and weather, the enemy would almost certainly learn about the plan. If the invasion didn't happen on June 6 the chance might be lost forever.

Ike slumped in his chair and bowed his head in thought. Unsure of what to do, he decided to table the decision for a few hours. At 3:30 a.m. on June 5, Ike gathered his team together for a final decision. He asked each man for his opinion, pacing the room as he listened to their thoughts. The meteorologist reported that there might be a clearing in the weather. Ike knew the weight of the fateful decision belonged solely to him.

"Okay, we'll go."

It was on.

The order of the day, which Ike had been drafting for weeks, was distributed to the forces:

Soldiers, Sailors and Airmen of the Allied Expeditionary Forces:
You are about to embark upon the Great Crusade, toward which we have striven these many months. The eyes of the world are upon you. The hopes and prayers of liberty-loving people everywhere march with you. In company with our brave Allies and brothers-in-arms on other Fronts you will bring about the destruction of the German war machine, the elimination of Nazi tyranny

over oppressed peoples of Europe, and security for
ourselves in the free world . . .

That day, in a private moment, Ike scribbled a note to himself, which he put in his wallet. He meant for it to be distributed in the event the invasion failed. It said, in part, "I have withdrawn the troops. My decision to attack at this time and place was based upon the best information available. The troops, the air, and the navy did all that Bravery and devotion to duty could do. If any blame attaches to the attempt it is mine alone."

That evening, Eisenhower drove fifty miles to Newbury, where the 101st Airborne Division was preparing to start the first wave of the attack. Ike's feeling for his troops was always plain to see and heartfelt. He stayed with them until the last were in the air about midnight. Then he returned to camp to wait for the first news of the assault to come in.

Hours later, Eisenhower learned that the mission succeeded, but the loss of life was horrendous. Nearly 10,000 men died that day, and thousands more were wounded. But the Allies gained a crucial foothold that ultimately won the war.

The weather had been foul. The choppy seas proved so fierce that many men drowned before they reached the beaches. These poor conditions offered one benefit: the German commanders were caught unaware because they did not think the Allies would dare conduct a mission in such harsh weather. As it turned out, the weather would have been even worse if Eisenhower had decided to delay the invasion by two weeks.

Ike never bragged about the accomplishments of D-Day. For him it was a matter of duty. When Mamie asked him, "How in the world did you have the nerve to do this?" he replied, "I had to."

WINNING THE WAR

Although D-Day was a turning point toward Allied victory, it was followed by almost a year of the most brutal battles of the war. The Germans never let up. The most vicious German response came on December 16, 1944, as the Allies moved into Belgium. In a surprise attack in the forested land of the Ardennes region, more than 250,000 German forces overwhelmed 80,000 American forces in what became known as the Battle of the Bulge. Terrible weather made an American air assault impossible, and the forces were stranded and surrounded by the enemy.

Ike acted quickly to send in reinforcements. He called together a number of his generals, and attempted to lift their demoralized spirits with these words: "The present situation is to be regarded as an opportunity for us and not a disaster. There will be only cheerful faces at this table." With defeat a possibility, the men mapped out a strategy that could overwhelm and surround the Germans.

The Germans moved fifty miles beyond the American line before the Allied forces stopped their advance. At that time, the weather cleared and an aggressive air bombardment ended the German effort. The casualties were high—more than 20,000 Americans died, 43,000 were wounded, and 23,000 were captured or missing.

It was the final major assault of the war. Within months the Allied victory was complete. VE Day—Victory in Europe Day—was celebrated on May 8, 1945. President Roosevelt had died suddenly in April; in July President Harry Truman joined Josef Stalin and Winston Churchill to hammer out the details of the end of the war.

Ike met with President Truman to discuss what might come next. "General, there is nothing that you may want that I won't try to help you get," Truman told Eisenhower. "That definitely and specifically includes the presidency in 1948."

Ike laughed at the idea and assured Truman he had no interest in politics. That day, he had other pressing matters on his mind. Earlier, Secretary of War Henry Stimson had come to see him at his headquarters in Germany to deliver the news that the United States was planning to drop an atomic bomb on Japanese cities. The idea sickened Ike.

"I voiced to him my grave misgivings," Ike wrote, "first on the basis of my belief that Japan was already defeated and that dropping the bomb was completely unnecessary, and secondly because I thought that our country should avoid shocking world opinion by the use of a weapon whose employment was, I thought, no longer mandatory as a measure to save American lives."

No one listened. The bombs—one on Hiroshima and one on Nagasaki—fell about a week later.

The use of atomic bombs haunted Ike's thoughts throughout his presidency, right to the moment of his final address.

4

A NONPOLITICIAN RUNS FOR PRESIDENT

WHEN GENERAL DWIGHT D. Eisenhower returned to the United States after the war, he was welcomed with a ticker-tape parade in New York City. New York governor Thomas Dewey sat next to Ike at a dinner following the parade, and he became convinced that the general possessed all the qualities needed for the presidency. "I felt that the Republican Party was weak with the electorate and that a new style of candidate was the only sure way to win," Dewey said. "I was confident that General Eisenhower would win."

Eisenhower's standing in the world was at its peak. He had just coordinated the military mission that defeated

Hitler and saved the free world. He had a warm personality and the ability to charm people. The only problem was that Ike didn't think of himself as a politician.

Still, the drumbeat for Eisenhower to run for president did not let up, despite the fact that he had never even revealed his political party affiliation. In 1947, President Truman once again encouraged Ike to run for president, saying he'd consider not running for reelection in 1948 if the general would carry the Democratic banner. Truman assumed Ike was a Democrat. Ike politely declined.

BUILDING A GLOBAL COALITION

After the war, Eisenhower served as chief of staff of the U.S. Army for several years. Then, in 1948, his career took a turn when he accepted a position as president of Columbia University. He had retired from active service in the military, and he was testing the idea of a postmilitary career. At first, Ike thought the presidency of such an esteemed institution was out of his league, more suited to a scholar than a soldier. But the university directors wanted Ike, no doubt for his reputation and fund-raising ability. Once Ike got his mind around the idea, he thought about the ways he could make a difference to the students.

Ike took the job, and the Eisenhowers enjoyed their life in Manhattan. He continued to return to

Washington as a consultant to the Joint Chiefs of Staff when needed. In 1950, the nation was drawn back into war. Since the end of World War II, the Korean Peninsula had been unstable. Before World War II, Korea had been under Japanese rule; after the war, the United States and the Soviet Union had divided Korea, with the Soviets taking the North and the United States taking the South.

From the beginning, tensions ran high between the Soviet-backed People's Republic of Korea and the Western-supported government of South Korea. On June 25, 1950, troops from the North invaded South Korea with the goal of unifying the country under communist rule. The United Nations passed a resolution calling on the support of member nations, and sixteen countries sent troops to support South Korea, a majority of them being American soldiers.

In October 1950, President Truman contacted Eisenhower and told him he was needed to take command of the NATO forces in Paris. The combined forces had unanimously decided that the commander should be American—and it should be Eisenhower.

Ike accepted the post. In February 1951, Ike and Mamie moved to Paris. During this time, a growing number of people from both parties again called for Ike to consider a presidential run. Massachusetts senator

Henry Cabot Lodge Jr. pushed for an Eisenhower candidacy, often visiting Ike at NATO headquarters to make his case. The savvy politician saw in Ike the promise of the future. Ike represented a new, much-needed change in the character of politics. Americans loved him. People felt they *knew* him.

Ike began to soften to the idea when he considered the stakes. During his time as military commander of NATO, Ike became convinced that America needed to play a central role in global affairs. His turning point may have come during a conversation Eisenhower had with Robert A. Taft of Ohio, the son of William Howard Taft, the twenty-seventh president, and the Republican Party's leading candidate for the 1952 presidential nomination. As the two men talked about domestic policy, they were mostly in agreement. But when they discussed foreign policy, Taft favored an isolationist approach. Taft had been one of the loudest voices in protest of America's entry into the war against Nazism, and he was an opponent of NATO. Taft didn't believe America should get involved in global affairs.

Eisenhower couldn't have disagreed more. He believed the United States should play a strong leadership role in the world, especially where foreign powers had access to nuclear weapons.

Ike began to consider whether he should step into the

presidential race. "He was absolutely devoted to doing anything he could to bring us a little closer to peace in the world," said Milton Eisenhower, Ike's brother. The politicians urging him to run believed that Ike could win. Ike was more focused on whether he could make a difference if he won, and he wasn't ready to make a decision.

One of Ike's most dedicated supporters was Sherman Adams, the governor of New Hampshire. When Adams had first approached Eisenhower about running, Ike said, "You know, Governor, there isn't anything this country can give me that it hasn't given me. I've had the greatest opportunity of any citizen in history in respect to the things I've been engaged in. I have no interest in politics. It nauseates me."

Adams kept after him. He still thought Ike was the right man to run. Adams broke with the pro-Taft forces in his state and endorsed Ike. He and Lodge put Eisenhower's name on the ballot in the New Hampshire primary without his permission, creating momentum for an Eisenhower run.

In February 1952, a Draft Eisenhower rally at New York's Madison Square Garden drew 25,000 people. When Ike was shown a film of the event a few days later, his eyes filled with tears. Simply put, people liked Ike— more than that, they trusted him. "They knew that he was honest," said Milton. "They knew he was a man of integrity."

Gradually, Ike refined his political views. By the time he finally announced his candidacy, Ike revealed something few people knew until then—he had been a lifelong Republican. Many within the Democratic Party were bitterly disappointed to learn that Ike wouldn't be their man.

IKE FOR PRESIDENT

Ike made his decision to run for president in March 1952. He immediately resigned his position as NATO commander and formally left the army. He delivered the announcement in Abilene in the midst of a driving rain, with his pants rolled up to keep them out of the mud.

Eisenhower was not a natural politician. Campaigning did not come easily to him. With all the clamor for Ike, it might seem that he was a shoo-in to win the nomination, but that wasn't the case.

Going into the convention in Chicago, Robert Taft had the lead. Ike was a latecomer. On the eve of the convention, the Associated Press reported that of the 604 delegates needed for nomination, Taft had 530 and Ike had 427. Of the remaining delegates, California governor Earl Warren held 76, and former governor of Minnesota Harold Stassen had 25.

Taft was a seasoned politician who also represented the conservative wing of the party. But many in the party had more confidence that Ike could *win* in November's general election. He also had the media behind him. The *New York Times* argued against Taft on the grounds that Republicans needed to gain support from Democrats and independents in order to win back the White House, which had been in Democratic hands since 1933.

At the convention, Ike's forces aggressively challenged pro-Taft delegates in several states, claiming Eisenhower voters didn't get fair treatment. They put forth a rules challenge called the "Fair Play" rule, stating that these challenged delegates should not be allowed to participate in roll call votes. After a heated debate, the contested delegates broke for Ike, and voting on the first ballot showed him falling just short of the magic number, with 595 votes. In a dramatic move, Stassen rose to announce Minnesota would switch its votes to Eisenhower, and others followed. In the end, Ike won a decisive victory, with 845 votes to Taft's 280.

Ike's first act as Republican nominee was to embrace his rival. He rushed across the street from his hotel to where Taft was staying. When reporters called after him, "Where are you going?" he replied, "Where am I going? I'm going across the street and say hello to

Mr. Taft. I just called him and asked if I could come over." Taft swallowed his disappointment and shock and appeared jointly with Ike in an appeal to party unity. Taft returned to the Senate, and he and Ike became friends and golfing partners in spite of their political differences.

In the selection of a vice president, Ike listened to advisors, who were urging him to choose Senator Richard Nixon from California. He didn't know Nixon well but liked his youthful energy; Nixon was thirty-nine at the time. The Republican ticket was ready to go.

Two weeks later, the Democrats gathered and nominated Illinois governor Adlai Stevenson as their presidential candidate. Stevenson was a popular governor, but he was weak on the international stage. He was also virtually unknown outside his home state, while almost everyone knew Ike.

ON THE CAMPAIGN TRAIL

Ike was surprised by the bureaucracies of the campaign trail. Before a trip to Philadelphia, he was handed a thirty-five-page set of logistics. He laughed. "Politics is a funny thing," he said. "Thirty-five pages to get me into Philadelphia. The invasion of Normandy was on five pages."

Eisenhower's fresh approach to politics meant he did things differently. It had been assumed that the South "belonged" to Democrats, so he should just write it off.

When advisors told Ike that he was not campaigning in the South, he pushed back.

"What do you mean I'm not going into the South?" he asked. "I'm running for president of all the country, aren't I?" In his best general's voice, he said, "I'll tell you, gentlemen, I'm going to go into the South right after Labor Day." And he did, traveling to Atlanta, Birmingham, Little Rock, and Tampa, among other cities. There were big crowds at every stop.

It ended up being a masterful play because the Democrats hadn't planned on spending much time in the South. With Ike campaigning in the typically Democratic stronghold, Stevenson was forced to devote more time there than he'd wanted to. So, in doing the right thing, Ike also made a *politically* wise choice.

But Ike didn't always get it right. His political inexperience was responsible for one of the most unpleasant episodes on the campaign trail. In 1952, Joseph McCarthy's communist witch hunt was reaching full steam, and one of his targets was Ike's old boss, General George Marshall. Marshall had served as secretary of state and secretary of defense in the Truman administration and was author of the Marshall Plan, the economic aid program that rebuilt Western Europe after World War II. McCarthy said the Marshall Plan aided America's enemies and Marshall was "eager to play the role of a front man to traitors." He accused Marshall of working with Stalin in "a conspiracy on a scale so immense as to dwarf any previous such venture in the history of man."

Ike was enraged by the accusations. On a campaign trip to McCarthy's home state of Wisconsin, Ike planned to give a speech in which he praised Marshall as a patriot. McCarthy was supposed to be in the audience in Milwaukee that night. Shortly before the speech, Republican leaders urged Ike not to challenge McCarthy in his home state.

Ike cut the paragraph about General Marshall out of his speech. He did not defend his friend, who he knew was being falsely accused.

Truman attacked Eisenhower for his decision, charging that Ike of all people should be willing to openly defend Marshall. "I had never thought the man who is now the Republican candidate would stoop so low," Truman said. "A man who betrays his friends in such a fashion is not to be trusted with the great office of president of the United States."

Privately, Ike agonized over what he knew had been a mistake. In 1952, the Red Scare created panic. In this case, politics won out over personal loyalty, and it was a rare stain on Ike's record of authenticity.

It wasn't just the McCarthy incident that bothered Truman. The president felt betrayed when Ike aggressively campaigned against his administration. He took it personally. When Democratic candidate Stevenson said, "I will clean up the mess in Washington," Ike seized on the line, saying the two sides had that much in common. At the White House, Truman fumed.

Another incident almost derailed Ike's campaign. Just before Ike was going to deliver a speech about honesty in government, the news broke that his running mate, Richard Nixon, had used campaign funds for personal expenses. Integrity was absolute for Ike, but he ignored cries to "throw him off the ticket" and waited for Nixon to respond.

In a career-saving television speech, Nixon defended his integrity and spoke of his Middle American values. The winning remark was a comment Nixon made about his family's beloved dog, Checkers, a gift to his children. This became known as the Checkers speech. It worked—the American people forgave him—but Ike never quite felt at ease with Nixon, whom he considered "too political."

Ike continued to work the campaign trail. He made many short speeches—sometimes as many as twelve a day—from the caboose platform of his campaign train as it powered across America. He enjoyed using props to demonstrate the inefficiency of the federal government. One of these was a piece of lumber about four feet long, sawed almost completely through in two places. He'd hold up the wood and tell the crowd how in a previous time they could buy this strip of lumber for twenty-five cents. Then he'd break it over his knee at the first sawed place and hold it up again, saying, this was how much you could buy for twenty-five cents a few years earlier. Finally, he'd break it again and say that this is what twenty-five cents would buy in 1952. This visual trick was a crowd-pleaser, an effective way of showing an economic fact his audience could relate to.

Eisenhower wanted to attract all voters, not just Republicans. Many of his rallies were organized by Citizens for Eisenhower, a group not affiliated with the Republican Party. That way people didn't have to sign on as Republicans to support him. They could just be for the candidate, not the party.

Songwriter Irving Berlin wrote a campaign song, "I Like Ike." Walt Disney Studios made an animated campaign ad using the song with different lyrics. The catchy tune struck a cheerful note, like a popular commercial jingle:

You like Ike
I like Ike
Everybody likes Ike for president
Hang out the banner
Beat the drums
Let's take Ike to Washington

Many Americans were concerned about the war in Korea. In October, just weeks before the election, Eisenhower dramatically announced, "I shall go to Korea." He was a famed general and the public believed he could put an end to the conflict in Korea. The American people had faith that Ike was capable of doing the impossible in times of war, and they had hope that he could end the crippling standoff.

AN ELECTION VICTORY

On the eve of the election, November 3, the Republican National Committee and the Citizens Committee for Eisenhower and Nixon aired an hour-long television program promoting Eisenhower. It was different from anything viewers had seen before. It opened with a cozy scene in a living room with two couples—Ike and Mamie Eisenhower and Richard and Pat Nixon—seated around a television set. They smiled into the camera and told viewers that they didn't know anything about the program but were going to watch along with the American public. What followed was a love letter to Ike, as ordinary citizens and campaign workers from across the country praised the general and spoke of their hopes for the future.

November 4, 1952, was the first nationally televised coverage of election returns. The process of determining the winners in political races used to be much more difficult and time-consuming. That night, as Walter Cronkite anchored election night coverage on CBS, he announced that a computer called Univac would be predicting the results. Cronkite didn't trust the computer, and when very early in the evening it predicted an Eisenhower landslide, he held back the results. Later that night it was clear that the computer was right. Eisenhower won a solid victory with 55 percent of the popular vote and a landslide in the Electoral College, with 442 votes to Stevenson's 89. He even did well in the South.

The election was a referendum on the Democratic Party, which had been in power for a long time. Republicans won control of Congress as well, although by slim margins. In Massachusetts, Henry Cabot Lodge Jr. lost his Senate seat to a newcomer named John F. Kennedy.

President Truman wrote a cool note of congratulations to Ike. The two men met at the White House for a brief meeting that did nothing to heal the hostility between them. Their wives were warmer. Bess Truman invited Mamie to the White House to look around, and she accepted. Bess greeted her excitedly. "Oh, Mrs. Eisenhower," Bess said, "I want to show you—I picked out the most wonderful suite for the grandchildren!" Mamie was touched by the thoughtful gesture. She had been concerned about making the White House a welcoming place for her grandchildren.

As president-elect, Ike had trouble learning to work with the Secret Service. Without consulting them, he had arranged a trip to Korea. The head of the Secret Service called him: Didn't Ike realize that by law the Secret Service was required to be with him at all times? Reluctantly, Ike agreed to have one agent with him on the plane, with others traveling on a second plane.

The trip to Korea stirred up more trouble with Truman. General MacArthur, who had been ousted from Truman's administration over their disagreement about the handling of the war, said in a speech that he had a "clear and definite solution to the Korean conflict." Ike was eager to hear what MacArthur had to say. He wrote a message to the general: "I appreciate your announced readiness to discuss these matters with me and assure you I am looking forward to informal meetings in which my associates and I may obtain the full benefit of your thinking and experience."

MacArthur responded: "This is the first time that the slightest official interest in my counsel has been evidenced since my return."

Ike released the communications to the press, and Truman was furious. Truman responded by lashing out at both Eisenhower and MacArthur, saying that if MacArthur had a plan to end the war, he had a duty to present it to the president. Truman also called Ike's

Korea trip a political stunt, which angered the president-elect.

In Ike's opinion, the Korean War was being mismanaged. More than two years in, with negotiations at a standstill, Ike believed the parents and families of the men fighting would be sickened to hear how vulnerable American forces were in the face of attacks from the North. When he visited the country, he learned how bad things really were. It was a hard trip, involving traveling miles by jeep and riding in small planes in freezing weather, but that was the only way for Ike to learn the truth about the war. He was outraged to find that the North Koreans, now supported by the Chinese, shelled the troops every day, while American soldiers were under orders not to fire back.

Eisenhower was president-elect, but in Korea everyone saw him as General Eisenhower. He warned that unless there was an agreement to sit down and work out an immediate truce, the war would resume full force. Moved by what he saw in Korea, and determined to end the war once he assumed office, Ike returned to the United States to prepare for his inauguration.

GENTLE BUT STRONG
JANUARY 20, 1953
INAUGURATION DAY

PRESIDENT HARRY TRUMAN AND President-Elect Dwight Eisenhower rode in the limousine to the inauguration ceremony in stony silence. As they neared the Capitol, Ike tried to break the tension by asking Truman who had ordered his son, Army Major John Eisenhower, home from Korea for the inauguration.

"I did," Truman said.

Ike thanked him sincerely.

Truman let the silence return, so Ike tried to start the conversation again. He said that in 1948 he had decided not to attend Truman's inauguration because he didn't want any publicity that might distract from the president's big moment.

Unmoved, Truman said that Eisenhower wasn't there because he hadn't been invited. "If I'd told you to come, you would have been there," Truman said.

The two men rode the rest of the way in silence.

At noon, Eisenhower placed his hand on top of two Bibles—the one his mother had given him when he graduated from West Point and the Bible George Washington used for his oath as the nation's first president. Standing next to two past presidents, Harry Truman and Herbert Hoover, Eisenhower was sworn in as the thirty-fourth president of the United States. When he was finished, he turned and kissed Mamie, the first inaugural kiss in American history.

As Ike stepped to the podium to deliver his inaugural address a few minutes later, he looked out on the crowds and hoped to speak from the heart. He had struggled through several drafts of his speech, but they hadn't felt right. Finally, on Inauguration Day itself, Ike decided that what he needed was an opening prayer. He asked everyone to bow their heads and he said: "Almighty God, as we stand here at this moment, my future associates in the executive branch of government join me in beseeching that Thou will make full and complete our dedication to the service of the people in this throng, and their fellow citizens everywhere." Those opening words grounded the new president in his humble call to faith and action.

After the ceremony, Ike and Mamie attended a luncheon sponsored by the Joint Congressional Committee on Inaugural Ceremonies. It was the first official inaugural luncheon, but the event was successful and became a tradition. Following lunch, the presidential couple rode down Pennsylvania Avenue in a white Cadillac convertible. An estimated 750,000 people jammed the parade route between the Capitol and the White House. Ike and Mamie sat in the viewing stand in front of the White House and watched 22,000 servicemen, parade floats, musical acts, horses, and three elephants march past during a four-and-a-half-hour parade.

That night, the Eisenhowers attended two lavish inaugural balls. Originally, there had been only one ball planned, but the demand for tickets was so great that a second event had to be added. Once the special events were over, Ike put on his old brown bathrobe and sat in his bedroom talking to his son, John. They did not wander through the White House, marveling at the history. Instead, Ike spent his first night as president being a father to the son, who would soon return to his post in Korea.

IKE BUILDS HIS TEAM

Truman had a plaque reading "The Buck Stops Here" on his desk in the Oval Office. Ike had a paperweight on his desk etched with the Latin words *Suaviter in modo, fortiter in re*: "Gently in manner, strong in deed." Those words summed up Eisenhower's core philosophy. He wanted to use his power as president to be a calming influence in a mixed-up world.

As he set up his administration, Ike looked for people he thought could get things done, rather than those with political connections. For example, he chose Charles Wilson, the former CEO of General Motors, as his secretary of defense. Ike knew from experience that the Pentagon was wasteful and inefficient, and he thought Wilson's management skills and strong personality could make the military more streamlined and effective.

In the same way, Ike's choice of George Humphrey as secretary of the treasury was pragmatic. Humphrey, a prominent businessman and chairman of the M. A. Hanna steelworks company, was well-positioned to oversee the economic direction of the nation. The new administration had inherited a $9 billion budget deficit and a fragile economy, and Ike felt confident in handing over these challenges to the mild-mannered midwesterner, who was a no-nonsense believer in the edict that people had to live within their means—and that included the government.

Ike had an eye for the doers, even if, like his choice for secretary of state, John Foster Dulles, they were not the most outgoing or popular. He had great admiration for Dulles, although the two men were never friendly. Dulles could be stuffy and impersonal in his dealings with people. But few questioned his penetrating clarity or experience, and he remained Ike's right hand until he was forced to resign in 1959 due to advancing colon cancer, which killed him months later.

Ike chose his campaign manager, Herbert Brownell Jr., for attorney general. Ike found much to like about Brownell. He had a warm personality, strong character, and sharp intellect. He also had a gift for empathy and would shepherd into law the first civil rights advances in eighty years.

Recognizing the importance of including women in leadership positions within his administration, Ike appointed Oveta Culp Hobby—the woman who founded the Women's Army Auxiliary Corps in World War II—as the head of the Federal Security Agency. It wasn't a cabinet position, but she sat in on cabinet meetings. In 1955, Hobby was appointed secretary of the newly formed Department of Health, Education, and Welfare, becoming the second woman to sit on a presidential cabinet—the first being Frances Perkins, who served as secretary of labor under Franklin Roosevelt.

Ike felt especially close to James Hagerty, his campaign press secretary and right-hand man, and he brought him into the administration as press secretary. He also chose another supporter, Sherman Adams, for chief of staff, which was a new role then. He'd considered appointing a military officer but feared it would look as if he were trying to set up a military operation. Adams had once been referred to as a New Hampshire "chunk of granite."

Eisenhower encouraged collaboration and communication in his cabinet meetings. He insisted people speak freely and expected them to be ready to explain and defend their opinions. Ike maintained an open-door policy and made time for people who wanted to see him. He genuinely cared what those around him thought about the issues.

IKE'S "HIDDEN HAND"

Eisenhower often joked that he considered the ability to play bridge a key qualification for any of his top aides. Bridge is a game of secrets and strategy, and it's not surprising Ike was a skilled player.

The aspect of Ike's character that allowed him to excel at bridge—and in war and government—is called the "hidden hand," a term coined by political scientist Fred I. Greenstein. Greenstein wrote of Ike's ability to act while masking his underlying intentions. Ike did this by downplaying his skill as a politician and convincing the American people that he was above politics. He never attacked people personally, so he maintained his public image as a likable, goodhearted person. When it suited him, he used ambiguous language so that he couldn't be pinned down about *exactly* what he meant. In addition, Ike was able to distance himself from difficult issues by giving those who worked for him important assignments—but he never lost control of policy.

The downside to Ike's hidden-hand approach was that he could sometimes appear indecisive and weak instead of cautious and thoughtful. One important example was how he handled Wisconsin senator Joseph McCarthy and his hunt for communists in the government. McCarthy had only grown stronger since Ike's first unpleasant encounter with him in the election. Things came to a head in 1954 when McCarthy accused several members of the army of being communist sympathizers. Ike was enraged at the slanderous remarks, but he didn't act. "You can't defeat Communism by destroying America," the president said. But he refused to "get down in the gutter with that guy."

Ike hoped his silence would starve McCarthy of the publicity he craved. He didn't think the president of the United States should get into a shouting match with a junior senator from Wisconsin. Ike's cautious approach drew criticism, including from his brother Milton.

Although the president did not like to play politics, he

knew knocking out McCarthy might put the Republican majority in jeopardy. And the Red Scare had some momentum with the public. So it was a tricky matter. Still, with his attacks on army patriots, McCarthy was getting to be too much for Ike to endure, and he began a steady backroom campaign against him. In a meeting with the legislative leadership, Ike urged them to rein McCarthy in. Privately, the president was in a rage. Pacing angrily in his office, he exploded to Hagerty, calling McCarthy's actions "the most disloyal" ever seen by anyone in the government of the United States.

Then, in a speech at Columbia University's Bicentennial Dinner on May 31, he spoke plainly about those who would confuse "honest dissent with disloyal subversion." He never mentioned McCarthy's name, but the audience, interrupting the speech frequently with loud applause, got the point. "Through knowledge and understanding we will drive from the temple of freedom all those who seek to establish over us thought control," Ike said as the crowd cheered, "whether they be agents of a foreign state or demagogues thirsty for personal power and public notice." There was no doubt who he was talking about.

Things came to a head in the Army–McCarthy hearings on June 9 when a furious McCarthy named a young man in the office of Joseph Welch, the special counsel to the army, as having communist affiliations. The moment broke a years-long spell when Welch responded in quiet but burning anger, calling out McCarthy's tactics with words that would resonate down through the decades: "Until this moment, Senator, I think I never really gauged your cruelty or your recklessness. Have you no sense of decency, sir?" The hearing room erupted in cheers.

History has deemed Welch's rebuke as the moment that brought McCarthy down. It is less certain of Ike's role. While it is probably true the president's behind-the-scenes efforts hastened McCarthy's demise, to those who were hunted and ruined by his demagoguery, in hindsight it was a slow death where a more rapid and brutal end was called for.

A HEART ATTACK AND RECOVERY

On Friday, September 23, 1955, Ike was in Denver on a four-day fishing trip. For lunch he had a hamburger with onions and a pot of coffee. He suffered digestive pain all afternoon and still felt sick when he went to bed, but he didn't think it was anything serious. He woke up at 1:30 a.m. with chest and stomach pains. He told Mamie he needed milk of magnesia, and she called for his personal physician.

Instead of sending the president to the hospital, his

doctor treated him with medication and sent him back to bed. The pain continued in the morning, so he went to the hospital, where an electrocardiogram showed the president had suffered a heart attack.

Long before the incident, Ike had told his staff that if he ever became ill, he wanted the details disclosed to the American people. As a result, the nation was fully briefed and rooted for Ike as he went through his health crisis. As was customary care at the time, Ike spent seven weeks in the hospital on bed rest.

Ike recovered from his heart attack, but he had to decide whether to run for reelection in 1956. He hosted a private dinner at the White House for his closest advisors and asked them to discuss the pros and cons of running for another term. His brother refused to weigh in, but the others thought he should run. They argued Ike was the only one who could work effectively to stop a world war and build the promise of peace.

In February 1956, Ike went to Walter Reed Army Medical Center for tests, and the doctors announced him well enough to take on a second term. His doctor said, "If you run I will vote for you." Ike decided to run. He had much still to do.

Ike easily won reelection. The Democrats again nominated Adlai Stevenson, who lost by a greater margin than he had in 1952. The only drama surrounded the vice-presidential contest on the Democratic side. In a fierce fight, Tennessee senator Estes Kefauver defeated Massachusetts senator John F. Kennedy on the third ballot. In the process, Kennedy achieved a national platform from which he would build a White House run four years later.

PROGRESS IN CIVIL RIGHTS

During his administration, Eisenhower helped to shape the civil rights movement in the United States. In his first year in office, Supreme Court Chief Justice Fred Vinson died, and Ike appointed Earl Warren to his seat. The Warren Court, which would last until Warren's retirement in 1969, would be activist on many issues. One of the most important decisions of the court was the 1954 ruling *Brown v. Board of Education*, which reversed the separate-but-equal doctrine and paved the way for school desegregation.

The court's ruling resulted in protests across the South. Many local officials refused to accept integration as the law of the land. After years of legal challenges, the final showdown came in September 1957 at Central High School in Little Rock, Arkansas. On the first day of school, nine African American students tried to enter the school, but they were blocked by protesters, then by police as ordered by the governor.

Ike considered it his job to enforce the law. The way he saw it, once the Supreme Court made its ruling and integration was settled law, it was his obligation to make sure the ruling was followed. Arkansas governor Orval Faubus mobilized the Arkansas National Guard to prevent the students from entering school, so Ike called Faubus to a meeting. Ike reminded the governor that desegregation was the law, and that the only legitimate use of the National Guard should be to escort the students into the school.

Faubus ignored the president, so Ike decided to send federal forces. Troops from the 101st Airborne descended on Arkansas and escorted the children to school.

Ike saw segregation not only as a domestic issue, but as a stain on America's reputation in the world. Addressing the nation from the Oval Office, Ike said, "I want to speak to you about the serious situation that has arisen in Little Rock. In that city, under the leadership of demagogic extremists, disorderly mobs have deliberately prevented the carrying out of proper orders from a federal court." He explained his decision to use federal troops to enforce the law.

"Our enemies are gloating over this incident and using it everywhere to misrepresent our whole nation," he said. "We are portrayed as a violator of those standards of conduct which the peoples of the world united to proclaim in the Charter of the United Nations." Afterward, the troops did their job, the mobs faded away, and the black students entered the school and began the business of education.

At the very moment he was going head-to-head with Orval Faubus, Ike signed the Civil Rights Act of 1957, the first civil rights legislation passed by Congress since 1875. The law offered some additional protections to black citizens to exercise their right to vote. Despite Ike's support of the law and his defense of the students in Little Rock, the president was criticized for not having been more outspoken and passionate in defense of desegregation at an earlier point in the debate. But what he lacked in fire, he more than made up for in action. It wasn't Ike's way to be dramatic, but in his steady, forceful way, he advanced the cause of civil rights.

THINKING AHEAD

In his final years in the White House, Ike was beginning to think about life after politics. He and Mamie had purchased a farm in Gettysburg a decade earlier and spent seven years renovating it. As his second term drew to a close, Ike looked forward to spending time on the farm with his family.

When looking at Eisenhower's presidency, the contradictions are notable, especially that he was a man of war who craved peace. Many people assumed that putting an army general in the White House would elevate the military class, but the opposite proved to be true. President Franklin D. Roosevelt had World War II. President Truman had the Korean War. President Kennedy had the Bay of Pigs invasion, and President Johnson had Vietnam. On the other hand, Eisenhower ended the Korean War and carried the country through two terms without engaging in another war.

Ike's passion for peace shaped his final days in office. Three days before the inauguration of John F. Kennedy, Eisenhower was determined to give the speech of his life. His words would be the culmination of all he had done and all he believed. It would not be just another speech, and certainly not a sentimental goodbye. Instead, in his final address, Ike wanted to stake out his position in history and once again warn his country about the hazards of war.

Part 2

THE SPEECH

6

GOOD EVENING, MY FELLOW AMERICANS
JANUARY 17, 1961
THE WHITE HOUSE

PRESIDENT DWIGHT EISENHOWER SAT at his desk in the Oval Office rewriting his farewell speech, even though it had already been copied for distribution to reporters. Reporters had learned from experience not to take the "official" version as final. No one knew exactly what the president was going to say until he took the microphone.

Ike had been at the final editing since before eight that morning. As he worked, he heard pounding and hammering as construction workers assembled the inaugural parade viewing stand outside his window.

He was watching the clock, knowing that the hour was nearing when the technicians would take the final draft to set up the teleprompter. (As it turned out, Ike disliked using a teleprompter. He kept a paper copy of his remarks on his desk and he referred to that, as needed.)

In 1961, television was still fairly new. Ike wasn't the perfect messenger for the television era, but he did his best. His friend Robert Montgomery, an Academy Award–winning actor who was active in Republican politics, often came to the White House to coach the president before a major speech. He wasn't trying to teach Ike how to act like a movie star; his goal was to help Ike be Ike.

At 8:30 p.m. that night, millions of Americans would turn on their televisions to watch the president say good-bye to the nation. The speech would take only a matter of minutes, but Ike had spent more than a year refining his message and choosing his words.

WRITING THE SPEECH

Ike began thinking about his farewell speech in the spring of 1959. He told his speechwriter Malcolm Moos to start considering themes and shaping some ideas for the final address. Ike wanted to get his message just right.

It wasn't easy being a speechwriter for Eisenhower. He

was an excellent writer himself, and he found pleasure in tearing apart early drafts. His brother Milton once joked that giving Ike a speech draft was like waving a red flag at a bull. It was an invitation to attack and tear apart. Ike always rewrote the manuscripts provided by his speechwriters, taking out fancy phrases and adding his plainspoken touches.

When people charged him with not writing his own speeches, Ike pushed back. "You know that General MacArthur got quite a reputation as a silver-tongued speaker when he was in the Philippines," the president said. "Who do you think wrote his speeches? *I* did."

Ike didn't just write his speeches, he rewrote them again and again. The farewell address had been rewritten almost thirty times since 1959. In the end, Ike rewrote the opening passages in his own hand just before it was time to make the speech.

When he began to think about the address, Ike knew he wanted to reflect on the need to unify America by making room in government for a broad range of political beliefs. He also considered it essential to comment on America's role in the world during the nuclear age. Moos presented draft after draft to Ike, who turned each one down. Finally, in early December 1960, Moos took a rough draft of the speech into the Oval Office for Eisenhower to read. This time Ike read it over and said,

"I think you've got something here." He slid it into his drawer to review later.

Most people didn't expect much from a retiring president's farewell address. Typically, such speeches were simple messages, sometimes sentimental, always dominated by bragging about the administration's accomplishments. If he'd wanted to, Ike could have boasted about his many achievements. He had ended the Korean War, ensured eight years of peace, created the Interstate Highway System, passed the first civil rights legislation since Reconstruction, and balanced several budgets. More importantly, he had been a careful leader who kept America safe in the nuclear age.

The 1950s had been a time of prosperity in America, characterized by growth, stability, and promise. The economy had grown nearly 40 percent and unemployment was low. The GI Bill—a law that gave millions of World War II veterans access to higher education and better jobs—helped create a stable middle class. Those who complained about how dull the Eisenhower years were may have forgotten the unemployment lines, military funerals, rationing, and hardships of the 1930s and 1940s. Those who endured the Great Depression and World War II no doubt welcomed this period of peace and prosperity.

But his speech would not focus on those achievements.

Instead, his thoughts were consumed by the challenges of the future.

CONCERNS ABOUT MILITARY MIGHT

Eisenhower was concerned with how America used its power in the world. He knew that his first obligation was to the American people, but he believed that the United States needed to be conscious of its role as a global superpower in the nuclear age. He worried that for the first time in history, the United States had a permanent war-based economy.

Eisenhower knew the United States had to maintain an arsenal of nuclear weapons. Only by having these weapons could the nation defend itself. And, more importantly, these weapons would deter war, because the use of nuclear arms would result in mutual destruction. But the problem had become more complicated than that. Businesses and industrial partners constantly tried to make more and better bombs, which would be used to defend the country and to make lots of money for the private companies. Ike thought the country needed to be careful to ensure that the nation's interests were not defined by these powerful business interests.

In an early draft of his speech he called this relationship the "military-industrial-scientific complex." He realized that science wasn't the issue, so he edited the phrase.

In another draft he wrote about the "military-industrial–congressional complex." Then he realized that he didn't want the issue to seem partisan, so he edited the phrase again.

Finally, he settled on the "military–industrial complex." His intent was to plead for balance—to avoid the temptation to feel that a spectacular and costly action could solve all of our problems. The nation was in an impatient mood. But patience was a virtue worth cherishing.

SAYING GOODBYE

In his final days in office, Ike thought about how he wanted to say goodbye to those who had worked to support his administration and those he dealt with on a daily basis. He wasn't an especially sentimental man, but it was hard not to reflect on the profound transition from commander in chief to private citizen. No president in his or her final days can be fully prepared for not being president any longer. Ike felt relief mixed with regret for what remained undone and sadness over the end of a grand adventure.

Eisenhower hosted a dinner party in the State Dining Room at the White House for sixty reporters and photographers who had covered him during his presidency. He'd always received mixed reviews from the press. As the first "television president," he opened up greater access to the public, but he tended to go over and around the White House press corps when it served his purpose. And, of course, he didn't have the riveting glamour of JFK, which seduced many in the media. Most reporters respected Hagerty, though, and acknowledged that he did a masterful job of keeping them in the loop.

At the party, James E. Warner of the *New York Herald Tribune* mentioned to Ike he'd been assigned to cover him on his trip back to Gettysburg after Kennedy's inauguration.

Ike was surprised. "Why in the world would anybody want to cover an old ex-president?" he asked.

"That's my assignment, sir," Warner replied.

Ike laughed and pumped Warner's hand. "Well, welcome to the Old Frontier," he said, playing off JFK's famous campaign slogan.

Ike wanted to acknowledge those who had worked with him closely over the years. "You've done so much for me. I'd like to do something for you, too," Ike said to his chief of staff, Jerry Persons, who had replaced Sherman Adams in 1958. "What would you like?"

Persons said he wanted a portrait—"*of* you, *by* you."

Persons knew that Ike enjoyed painting in his free time. The president usually painted country scenes of farms and barns, but Persons wanted a presidential self-portrait. Eisenhower laughed, but a few months later, he presented his former chief of staff with the painting he requested.

His closest advisors had become like friends, and in December he'd sent them a letter:

> *During my entire life until I came back from World War II as something of a VIP, I was known by my contemporaries as Ike. Whether or not the deep friendships I enjoy have had their beginnings in the anti or postwar period, I now demand as my right that you, starting January 21, 1961, address me by that nickname. No longer do I propose to be excluded from the privileges that other friends enjoy. With warm regard, as ever—Ike*

Shortly after 8 p.m., after eating dinner with Mamie and changing into a fresh suit, Ike walked into the Oval Office. The room had been transformed into a TV studio. Ike stepped over a tangle of electric cords and allowed a makeup artist to powder his face. He straightened his tie and took his place behind the desk. The spotlight was on. The teleprompter was in position. The president laid out the final version of his speech on the desk in front of him.

He looked down at the page and then into the camera.

The floor director counted down, "Five . . . four . . . three . . . two . . . ," and then motioned his hand forward toward the president.

"Good evening, my fellow Americans . . ."

WORKING TOGETHER

Our people expect their president and the Congress to
find essential agreement on questions of great moment.
—From Eisenhower's farewell address

PRESIDENT DWIGHT EISENHOWER DIDN'T want his farewell address to be partisan. He wanted to unify the
nation, rather than promote party politics. While his
final speech did deal with foreign affairs and the threats
around the world, he was also intent on addressing the
issue of how to run a country across party lines and ide-
ologies.

Eisenhower thought bipartisanship was undervalued.
Too often people viewed it as the wishy-washy behavior
of those who lack moral convictions. But Ike knew he
could get more done and pass more of his agenda with

the help of moderate Democrats.

Ike had lots of experience working with groups he didn't have much in common with to find common ground. For example, in World War II the United States worked with its Allies—including the Soviet Union—toward the shared goal of defeating Hitler and Nazi Germany. During the war years, Ike was able to set aside his disagreement with these countries to support the larger goal of winning the war. In peacetime, the differences between America and the Soviet Union became more apparent, as the United States tried to rebuild Europe based on democratic principles and the Soviets tried to dominate the so-called Eastern Bloc and promote communism.

In the spirit of bipartisanship, Eisenhower wanted to praise the cooperation of congressional Democrats during his farewell speech. He said: "In this final relationship, the Congress and the Administration have, on most vital issues, cooperated well, to serve the nation well rather than mere partisanship, and so have assured that the business of the nation should go forward. So, my official relationship with Congress ends in a feeling, on my part, of gratitude that we have been able to do so much together."

Early in his presidency, Ike had some difficulties with members of his own party. When he met with the

Republican House and Senate leaders for the first time, he assumed that they would develop a strategy to fulfill the promises they had made during the campaign. The members of Congress explained that those promises were made to get votes, not to set policy. Ike was shocked. He planned to follow through on those pledges. This was the kind of behavior that made Ike distrust— and dislike—politics. He was the first president since Ulysses Grant who had not previously been a member of Congress, a governor, or served in a president's cabinet. Without political experience, he was less familiar with the unspoken rules of politics. "Good man, but wrong business," said Speaker of the House Sam Rayburn when Ike was elected in 1952.

Despite this lack of political know-how, the Eisenhower years didn't have much political drama or angry partisanship, even though he was a Republican president with a Democratic Congress during six of the eight years of his presidency. In trying to explain his success working with the legislative branch, Ike zeroed in on two ideas: *interdependence* and *intimacy.*

In his farewell address, Eisenhower called for "interdependence." He wanted to quiet the isolationists and remind the nation that the United States had an important role to play on the world stage. Ike used the word "intimacy" to describe the bond he felt with lawmakers because of their shared American values.

Eisenhower first learned about the importance of a shared mission and common goal while fighting in wartime. As president, he again recognized the importance of having common goals in government. Ike believed that most congressional representatives were public servants at heart. While their short-term goals and philosophies might differ, their dedication to working for their country was honorable. Eisenhower sought common ground where he could find it, and he was quick to offer praise when it was earned. In his eight years as president, he resisted the temptation to blame Congress for his failures.

One of the best examples of Ike's talent for seeing the best in the people he disagreed with can be seen in his relationship with Robert Taft, his onetime political opponent. In spite of the strong differences between the two men regarding America's role in the world, Ike admired Taft as a smart and experienced public servant. Even when they didn't see eye to eye, the president considered Taft a decent man. From the beginning, Ike knew he needed to get along with his opponent if they were to accomplish anything. For the greater good, Eisenhower reached out to Taft and they made an uneasy peace, even playing golf on occasion. Sadly, the relationship didn't have a chance to flourish, as Taft died early in Ike's first term.

Eisenhower believed in collaboration. He made a commitment to listening to all members of Congress, even those who disagreed with him. Every Tuesday at 8:30 a.m., the president hosted a bipartisan meeting of members of Congress. Before the meeting, he would invite two lawmakers—one from the House of Representatives and one from the Senate, on a rotating basis—to have breakfast with him. In addition, Eisenhower held weekly meetings of the executive branch's departments and agencies on Saturday mornings. The goal was to encourage open communication and access to the president.

Ike believed it was in the interests of the nation for the president and Congress to get along. First and foremost, there were the shared goals of keeping the government running, supporting American interests abroad, and implementing the president's programs. The president remained a popular heroic figure with the public.

Eisenhower worked especially hard to develop and strengthen his relationships with Democratic congressional leaders Senator Lyndon Johnson and Representative Sam Rayburn. The men liked each other, and at least once a month they would have drinks together at the White House. They often had different political opinions, but they managed to get along.

Johnson seemed to Ike to be a purely ambitious

political animal. But he also had a refreshing streak of honesty. Early in their relationship, Johnson explained his rule of politics: "Mr. President, when I agree with you, I'll come tell you," he said. "I'll disagree with you with dignity and decency, and I won't talk about your dog or your boy."

In addition to politics, Johnson and Eisenhower shared the common experience of being heart attack survivors. On July 2, 1955, forty-six-year-old Johnson experienced cardiac arrest so severe it nearly killed him. Less than three months later, Ike suffered his heart attack. Both men resisted calls from friends and family to end their political careers. While Ike was in the hospital, Johnson sent him a note wishing him well and saying he'd recovered so completely from his own heart attack he'd gone hunting. In other words, he wanted to remind the president that they still had work to do.

By following this cooperative, bipartisan approach to government, Ike was able to make progress on significant issues of importance to the lives of Americans. While he didn't support the wild expansion of government programs, he did recognize the value of domestic programs and public works. He had no desire to do away with all of Franklin D. Roosevelt's New Deal programs. He did want to find a way to cut programs where he could to save taxpayers money, as well as to propose new programs when necessary. He always tried to be sensitive to what the American people wanted and expected.

One of Eisenhower's landmark pieces of legislation was the Federal-Aid Highway Act of 1956, which created the country's modern transportation infrastructure. This highway bill changed the nation, opening a new way of being defined by the open road. It took Eisenhower two years of unending effort to pass the bill, which was the biggest public works project in United States history at the time. In the end, it took a strong bipartisan coalition to get the legislation through Congress. Today, the Interstate Highway System is the backbone of America's infrastructure. The U.S. economy and way of life are unimaginable without the Eisenhower-era arteries that connect Americans from coast to coast.

NATION ABOVE PARTY

Republicans weren't always so happy with Ike's bipartisan approach. They thought he wasn't interested enough in party building. Ike did care about his party and he stumped for Republican candidates, but he thought it was more important to support the needs of the nation over the needs of his political party.

Eisenhower also refused to make political appointments based on party loyalty alone. When asked to fill a vacancy on a federal court, Ike demanded to see only candidates recommended by the American Bar Association, not political hacks.

In his farewell speech, Ike chose his words carefully, aiming his message, at least in part, at president-elect Kennedy. He wanted to tell the incoming president that seeking unity was not a sign of weakness. He offered a message that went beyond politics and politicians.

"The problems a president faces are soul-racking," Eisenhower once wrote. "The nakedness of the battlefield, when the soldier is all alone in the smoke and the clamor and the terror of war, is comparable to the loneliness—at times—of the presidency, when one man must conscientiously, deliberately, prayerfully scrutinize every argument, every proposal, every prediction, every alternative, every probable outcome of his action, and then—all alone—make his decision. All alone—because just when a new president needs allies, his circle of trust shrinks. No one, with the possible exception of his family, treats him the same, and no one, with the exception of his predecessors, knows what it is like."

In his closing words, he felt again the power of that revelation. He hoped his young successor would listen.

DEALING WITH THE SOVIET UNION

We face a hostile ideology global in scope.

—From Eisenhower's farewell address

PRESIDENT DWIGHT EISENHOWER FACED the White House press corps for the last time on January 18, 1961, the day after he delivered his farewell address and two days before he left office. When he was asked to name the greatest disappointment of his presidency, without hesitation he said it was his failure to achieve "a permanent peace with justice."

As president, Eisenhower had wanted to build a peaceful world. He had hoped to light a torch for peace that would, in his own words, "flame brightly until at last the darkness is no more." Although he had done his best, he had not been able to make that happen. Ike had withdrawn American troops from Korea and kept the United States out of new wars, but he felt uneasy about the state of global affairs.

In his farewell address, Eisenhower tried to convey some hard truths to President-Elect John F. Kennedy. As he had told Kennedy at their private meeting the previous month, the president of the United States doesn't get many easy-to-solve problems. "If they're easy, they're solved down the government line," Ike said. "It's only the virtually impossible problems that come to the president's desk."

When he took office in 1953, Ike inherited a number of challenges, including the Cold War, an expression used to describe the hostile relationship between the Soviet Union and the United States. Although the two countries fought together against Hitler during World War II, after the war it became clear that the superpowers were far apart in fundamental principles. Once the fighting ended, Soviet premier Josef Stalin became an outspoken critic of any efforts of the free world to unite around common principles of peace and freedom. He was a ruthless dictator who opposed democracy.

Stalin believed that both of the world wars had been caused by capitalism. "The uneven development of capitalist countries usually leads, in the course of time, to a sharp disturbance of the equilibrium within the world system of capitalism," Stalin said in 1946. He claimed that this imbalance ultimately leads to war. In Stalin's view, Soviet communism was noble and transformative, a system not of private greed but of collective duty.

Eisenhower strongly opposed communism. During his presidential campaign, he spoke out against communists, calling them "barbarians" and warning that "hope for peace among men disappeared under the monstrous advance of communist tyranny."

While Eisenhower disagreed with the communist system, once he became president he sought to improve the relationship between the United States and the Soviet Union. A lifelong strategist and problem solver, Ike wondered how he could strengthen the bond between the countries. He believed the two nations could reach a common understanding. One idea he suggested was an exchange program in which 15,000 American university students would study in the Soviet Union, and the same number of Soviet students would study in the United States. Ike believed in these mutually beneficial programs. Despite the policies of their leaders, he recognized that the Soviet people wanted the same things in life that Americans wanted. Ike believed that all human beings craved peace and security and a way to make a living.

HOW TO DEAL WITH THE SOVIET UNION

When Ike was elected president in 1952, he read a report saying that Stalin wanted to meet with America's new president. Ike was cautious. When a reporter asked him if he would meet with the Soviet leader, Eisenhower chose his words very carefully. "I would meet anybody, anywhere, where I thought there was the slightest chance of doing any good," the president said, "as long as it was in keeping with what the American people expect of their chief executive."

As it turned out, the two leaders never had a chance to meet. Ten days later, Stalin suffered a stroke. Eisenhower offered his condolences. An official White House statement said: "The thoughts of America go out to all the people of the USSR—the men and women, the boys and girls—in the villages, cities, farms and factories of their homeland. They are the children of the same God who is the father of all peoples everywhere. And like all peoples, Russia's millions share our longing for a friendly and peaceful world."

The following day, Stalin died. Ike wasn't sure how to respond or who would take control in the Soviet Union. He saw this as a moment of opportunity and a chance for peace as long as both sides were dedicated to ending the arms race. On April 16, 1953, the president delivered a speech titled "The Chance for Peace," which stunned the nation and gave the world pause. He spoke before the American Society of Newspaper Editors in Washington, DC, and the remarks were broadcast over television and radio. The address is considered one of the most radical of the Cold War era.

In the speech, Ike warned of the need for caution when establishing military spending priorities. He addressed concerns that had been virtually ignored during and after the war years. He said, in part:

> *Every gun that is made, every warship launched, every rocket fired signified, in the final sense, a theft from those who hunger and are not fed, those who are cold and are not clothed. This world in arms is not spending money alone. It is spending the sweat of its laborers, the genius of its scientists, the hopes of its children. The cost of one modern heavy bomber is this: a modern brick school in more than thirty cities. It is two electric power plants, each serving a town of 60,000 population . . . We pay for a single fighter with a half-million bushels of wheat. We pay for a single destroyer with new homes that could have housed more than 8,000 people . . . This is not a way of life at all, in any true sense. Under the cloud of threatening war, it is humanity hanging from a cross of iron.*

Ike also called on the Soviet Union to join a global coalition based on freedom, peace, and nonaggression. It was a critical moment when it was possible for the two sides to come together. Ike wanted to reframe the arms race and negotiate a new kind of relationship with the Soviet Union now that Stalin was dead.

Most Cold War historians describe a hardened and inflexible relationship between the Soviet Union and the United States, a battle between the communist "evil empire" and the freedom-loving West. But during this moment, Eisenhower recognized a chance to improve the relationship.

Eisenhower wanted to soften the hard line drawn by President Harry Truman. In 1947, Truman had said, "It must be the policy of the United States to support free people who are resisting attempted subjugation by armed minorities and pressures." This approach put America and its interests directly in opposition to the Soviets.

Ike was more focused on peace than conflict. He had firsthand experience with war, and he had been intimately involved in making a fragile peace. Eisenhower wanted to strengthen that peace, so during the summer of his first year as president, he convened a study group to brainstorm ideas about foreign policy. Named Project Solarium—because the group met in the White House sun room—the group debated various ways to address Soviet expansionism.

After a few weeks of study and discussion, the group presented its findings to White House cabinet members, the Joint Chiefs of Staff, and other high-ranking government officials. In the end, Eisenhower favored containment, an effort to stop the spread of communism. He wanted to avoid war and to avoid a showdown with the Soviet Union. He urged all of those in his administration to look for nonmilitary ways to reach America's goals.

ENDING THE KOREAN WAR

In the early months of his presidency, Eisenhower focused much of his attention on ending the war in Korea. Polls in the spring of 1953 showed that a majority of Americans believed the Korean War was "not worth fighting." Two-thirds of Americans approved of armistice or ending the fighting in Korea.

Eisenhower examined the options. He considered—and rejected—the idea of launching an aggressive attack against North Korea. He refused to let the war drag on as it was going, so he decided that it would be best to end the fighting. He believed his election to the presidency created unease among North Korea's leaders, who may have presumed that the famous general might be more willing than the previous administrations to use extraordinary force—possibly nuclear force.

Eisenhower's decision to seek a truce with Korea did not sit well with Secretary of State John Foster Dulles, who believed that if the United States didn't act with force, the country would look weak. Ike didn't listen. He believed it was time for the United States to "make a serious bid for peace."

At first, Ike's proposal for peace wasn't supported by South Korean president Syngman Rhee. Only when the United States threatened to withdraw all American aid and military support from South Korea did he agree to go along with the plan. The truce was scheduled for Sunday, July 27.

The president announced the agreement in a speech that included President Lincoln's words of reconciliation, delivered at the end of his second inaugural address:

> *With malice toward none, with charity for all, with firmness in the right as God gives us to see the right, let us strive on to finish the work we are in, to bind up the nation's wounds, to care for him who shall have borne the battle and for his widow and his orphan, to do all which may achieve and cherish a just and lasting peace among ourselves and with all nations.*

At the last minute, Ike scribbled his own ending: "This is our resolve and our dedication."

Ending the Korean War was the greatest accomplishment of Ike's first year. As 1953 wrapped up, the nation was at peace. But the period of quiet did not last long. Southeast Asia was on the brink of communist expansion. The French were trying to take back colonial control of Vietnam, which they had lost after World War II. Communist North Vietnam was fighting against democratic South Vietnam, and the United States worried that this part of the world could fall to communist control. "You have a row of dominoes set up, you knock over the first one, and what will happen to the last one is a certainty that it will go over very quickly," Eisenhower said, explaining his fear that communism would spread throughout the region. But was that enough to warrant American intervention?

Ike wasn't interested in getting involved in another war. "I am not going to land any American troops in those jungles," he said.

John F. Kennedy, the young senator from Massachusetts, disagreed with Eisenhower. Instead, he favored intervention. "Vietnam represents the cornerstone of the free world in Southeast Asia," Kennedy said, urging United States involvement.

Although Ike rejected military intervention, he supported the French and helped bring about the unsatisfactory compromise of a divided Vietnam. Later he sent military advisors to the area, but he did not send troops.

A SOVIET POWER CHANGE

The political situation in the Soviet Union was also unstable. After Stalin died, there was a power struggle in the Soviet Union for two years. During this time, the United States wasn't quite sure who was in charge. Nikolai Bulganin was appointed premier, but Nikita Khrushchev emerged as a behind-the-scenes leader. Although Khrushchev would not officially become premier until 1958, White House officials believed he was pulling the strings much earlier.

In July 1955, Eisenhower attended the Geneva Summit with the prime minister of Great Britain, the prime minister of France, and the premier of the Soviet Union. Even during this meeting, the United States wasn't sure that Soviet premier Nikolai Bulganin was in charge. Nikita Khrushchev attended the meeting as well. Did they share power?

During the conference Ike made a bold recommendation that the United States and the Soviet Union should allow reconnaissance planes to fly over each other's countries. The proposal—which was known as Open Skies—offered a way to hold each other accountable to any arms accords they might make.

As they were walking out after the meeting, Khrushchev approached Ike and said, "No, no, no. That is a very bad idea." Ike later said that at that moment he knew Khrushchev was really the man in charge. The Open Skies program never got off the ground. But the Soviets did get what they wanted out of the meeting: they forced the Americans to talk to them as equal partners.

One of the most important issues involving United States and Soviet relations was the fate of East Germany. In the final days of World War II, Ike, as commander, made a decision that had had an impact on Cold War politics for decades to come. As the Allies moved into Germany, it was up to Ike to decide which country would take Berlin. He believed that his job as commander was to achieve a military victory in the most efficient way. British prime minister Winston Churchill originally wanted to take Berlin, but Ike estimated that sending the British military would mean an additional 50,000 casualties. The Russians were in a better position to take Berlin, and Eisenhower let them have it.

Many people considered this decision the event that started the Cold War. From that point forward, Russia dominated the East and the Americans and Europeans controlled the West, an arrangement that was doomed to conflict from the start. The West pursued reunification; the East sought domination.

KHRUSHCHEV VISITS AMERICA

Despite their political differences, the United States and the Soviet Union moved ahead on cultural exchanges. As part of the effort, a Soviet exhibition opened in New York City in June 1959, and an American display opened in Moscow a month later. Vice President Richard Nixon went to Moscow for a private showing with Khrushchev. The American showcase featured the wonders of the free enterprise system, designed to inspire envy among people living in the communist state. During their time together, Nixon and Khrushchev debated about the virtues of each system. The media called it the Kitchen Debate, because it took place in a model American kitchen. Back home, Americans thought Nixon had "won" the debate. But in Moscow, where viewers had watched on TV, the verdict was that Khrushchev had won.

Less than two months after Nixon's visit to Moscow, Khrushchev came to the United States. When the Soviet leader arrived in Washington, Ike wanted to show him the sights from a helicopter. At first, Khrushchev refused to fly, but Ike convinced him. Seated side by side, with Khrushchev's interpreter in front, the world leaders rose up off the South Lawn of the White House and flew over Washington and its suburbs. Khrushchev was very critical of what he saw. Pointing to the rows of single-family houses, he said, "We have apartments in

Russia; this is very inefficient." When Khrushchev saw the heavy automobile traffic, he said, "We have buses in Russia." He said nothing positive.

Khrushchev asked Ike's press secretary how he was going to report their meeting in the press. Hagerty replied, "All I can assure you is that you will get fair treatment in the American press as you visit our country."

"Yes," the Soviet leader said, "but what are you going to tell them to say?" Khrushchev refused to accept that the press representative of the president had no power over the press.

Later, Eisenhower and Khrushchev went to Camp David and had a surprisingly friendly meeting. Khrushchev told Ike he loved western movies. "When Stalin was still alive, we used to watch westerns all the time," the Soviet leader confessed. That night, the two men watched movies together.

Ike noted that when he and Khrushchev were alone, they spoke more openly. Khrushchev wanted to learn more about consumer goods, how the economy worked, how much clothing cost, and how the automobile industry operated. Ike found Khrushchev charming, with a good sense of humor.

After leaving Camp David, Khrushchev visited Ike's farm in Gettysburg and spent time with the president's grandchildren. David, who was eleven at the time, later recalled the impact Khrushchev's visit made on him: "The possibility of war with the Russians was something, as a child, that I can remember worrying about all the time. And suddenly the leader of it all, Nikita Khrushchev, in your wildest fantasy, is suddenly standing there in front of you, and he's not that much taller than you are."

In a press conference the following day, Khrushchev said that he had met the president's grandchildren and they had held a conference to discuss joining their grandfather on a tour of the Soviet Union. "At that conference with the president's grandchildren, they and I reach a unanimous decision that they certainly should come with the president."

Ike took Khrushchev's warmth and good humor at face value—at least for the moment. He tried to understand the appeal of communism. Communists were atheists—they did not believe in God—and the totalitarian philosophy did not respect human rights. What was its appeal? He knew that people were promised liberation in exchange for personal freedom, community at the expense of individuality. The way Ike saw the economics, communism sliced an ever-smaller pie into ever-smaller pieces, while capitalism created an ever-expanding pie.

After Khrushchev returned home, Eisenhower was optimistic about the possibility of holding future summits and taking steps to limit the arms race.

That changed abruptly on May 1, 1960, when a Soviet surface-to-air missile shot down an American spy plane over Sverdlovsk, Russia, and pilot Francis Gary Powers was captured. According to the Soviets, Powers confessed the plane was under the direction of the Central Intelligence Agency.

In fact, the United States had been flying U-2 spy planes over Russia to keep track of its military and missile development since 1956—and Khrushchev knew this. Before the Powers incident, the American planes had been too high to shoot down, and rather than admit they couldn't hit them, the Soviets had kept quiet about it.

The subject of spying never came up during the Camp David discussions. After the incident, Ike had to figure out what he was going to tell the American people. He wasn't eager to admit that spying was going on, but he didn't want to appear like a tired old man who didn't know what was happening in his own country.

In the end, Eisenhower delivered a forceful speech, declaring that the spy program was under his direction and approval. He defended the need for keeping an eye on America's enemies, citing Pearl Harbor. The Soviets also conducted espionage, he said. He offered no apologies, and his speech—honest and strong—was well received by the American people.

After the U-2 incident, Khrushchev closed down all talks. He withdrew his invitation for Ike and his family to visit Moscow. Powers was paraded before the public and put on trial in Moscow, where he was sentenced to ten years in prison, including seven years of hard labor. (Later, during Kennedy's second year in office, Powers was released as part of a prisoner exchange.) Khrushchev decided to freeze relations until the United States elected a new president. Ike was deeply disappointed. The Cold War continued.

The relationship with the Soviet Union was a significant theme in Eisenhower's farewell address. Despite eight years of steady effort on his part, the communist threat remained strong. He had not made progress with the Soviets, and Eisenhower doubted that President-Elect Kennedy would be able to do better.

Ike knew that success required nonmilitary solutions. He believed America's wealth and might were not the sole measures of its dominance on the world stage. He often cited America's moral center and spirit as the keys to its success. Ike urged the country to follow a long-term strategy in global affairs instead of bouncing from one military action to another.

This was a particularly strong warning from an old soldier who resisted sending troops onto new battlefields. Eisenhower was speaking to the nation, but his words were chosen for an audience of one, the president-elect. He knew that Kennedy was tempted to follow a more aggressive approach to fighting communism. Once in office, would Kennedy follow Ike's advice and take a more strategic view?

CONFRONTING THE NUCLEAR THREAT

Disarmament, with mutual honor and confidence,
is a continuing imperative. Together we must learn
how to compose difference, not with arms, but with
intellect and decent purpose. I wish I could say tonight
that a lasting peace is in sight.
—From Eisenhower's farewell address

DURING THE 1960 CAMPAIGN, John F. Kennedy claimed that the United States was falling behind the Soviet Union in the production of defensive weapons. In an attempt to make his opponent look weak, Kennedy pounded away at the so-called missile gap between the United States and the Soviet Union. "I don't want to be the president of a nation perishing under the mushroom cloud of a nuclear warhead," he said. "And I intend, if president, or if I continue in the Senate, to build the defenses which this country needs, and which freedom needs."

In truth, there was no missile gap, and Kennedy knew it. The Central Intelligence Agency had briefed the candidate on the number of missiles held by both countries. Kennedy knew that he was misrepresenting the truth during his campaign speeches, but that didn't stop him. The message made him look strong.

It was impossible for the average citizen to know whether the Soviet Union had stockpiled more missiles than the United States. But Kennedy's words were compelling, and they might have won him the election. After becoming president, Kennedy had to backtrack on his claims about the missile gap. Two weeks after taking office, Kennedy admitted to the American people that there was no missile gap.

This discussion of nuclear weapons for political advantage angered Dwight Eisenhower. He knew that America had enough weapons to defend itself. He also objected to the tough talk, believing that an issue as serious as nuclear war should be discussed in words that were more thoughtful and measured.

How does one defend a nation against nuclear attack? The day he took office, Eisenhower had noticed a locked drawer in his desk in the Oval Office. He asked for a key and inside the drawer he found a report, which had been commissioned by President Harry Truman, predicting a frightening arms race between the United States and the Soviet Union, involving thousands of nuclear weapons and the missiles that could carry them across the globe. The report concluded that in the event of a nuclear attack, most of the country would be a moonscape of radioactive ash.

Ike believed it was his obligation to help the American people understand the consequences of nuclear war. It was too important for locked drawers. He encouraged the report's author, physicist J. Robert Oppenheimer, "the father of the atomic bomb," to write an article on the topic, which was published in the July 1953 issue of *Foreign Affairs*.

"The very least we can say," Oppenheimer wrote, "is that, looking ten years ahead, it is likely to be small comfort that the Soviet Union is four years behind us, and small comfort that they are only about half as big as we are. The very least we can conclude is that our twenty-thousandth bomb, useful as it may be in filling the vast munitions pipelines of a great war, will not in any deep strategic sense offset their two-thousandth . . . We need to be clear that there will not be many great atomic wars for us, nor for our institutions. It is important that there not be one."

Eisenhower understood that Kennedy's focus on the missile gap missed the point. Both sides already had enough bombs to destroy the world. America's nuclear stockpile had grown from about 1,000 warheads to about 23,000 during Ike's presidency. The United States wouldn't be any safer by building more.

Soviet premier Nikita Khrushchev knew the arms race was pointless, too. At the 1955 Geneva Summit, sitting together after dinner one night, Ike and Khrushchev had an informal discussion about nuclear arms. Ike said, "Of course, this is something we can never resort to."

"I agree," said Khrushchev. "I understand completely, Mr. President. We get your dust, you get our dust, the winds blow around the world and nobody's safe."

"Yes," said Ike. "That's what it's all about."

Later, at Camp David, Khrushchev admitted he had always been haunted by Chairman Mao's 1957 speech at the Moscow Meeting of Representatives of Communist and Workers' Parties in Moscow. Mao said that if there were a nuclear war, there would be 50 million Americans and 50 million Russians left, but there would be 450 million Chinese survivors. Khrushchev knew there could be no winners in a nuclear war.

Eisenhower understood the problems with using nuclear weapons defensively. In a press conference about the rising tension with the Soviet Union over Berlin, a reporter asked, "If the Russians press us on Berlin, are you prepared to use nuclear weapons?"

"No," the president snapped. "You can't *defend* anything with nuclear weapons."

That's not to say the president was unwilling to use nuclear weapons, but it was always considered a last resort. The threat of nuclear war was itself a barrier to conflict.

From the beginning of his presidency, Ike tried to slow the arms race. He wondered if nuclear technology could be used for positive ends. On December 8, 1953, as his first year in office drew to a close, Eisenhower stood before a packed meeting of the United Nations General Assembly and gave a speech that would later be named "Atoms for Peace."

He began by reminding the audience that the United States had the ability to destroy any enemy who might attack the United States or its allies. Then he shifted his argument. "To stop there would be to accept helplessly the probability of civilization destroyed, the annihilation of the irreplaceable heritage of mankind handed down to us from generation to generation . . . Surely no sane member of the human race could discover victory in such desolation."

Instead, he suggested that the nations of the world

attempt to harness nuclear energy in a way that could do good for the world. To that end, he proposed the United States and the Soviet Union agree to deposit certain amounts of uranium into an international uranium bank. This would reduce the supplies for bombs and open up the potential for other nations to draw from the bank for peaceful purposes, such as medical research or the development of new energy sources. In addition to limiting nuclear weapons, the effort would show that the world powers in both the East and West were interested in peaceful problem solving.

Ike's speech was well received both in the United States and around the world. Instead of seeing nuclear materials only for use in weapons, there was now talk of possible breakthroughs in medicine, agriculture, space, energy, and other applications that might build civilization rather than destroy it. The proposal led to the creation of the International Atomic Energy Agency, which promoted cooperation in science and technology across all borders.

Ike believed in slow but steady progress. He saw the program as a tiny start in getting the Soviet Union to turn toward the peaceful uses of atomic materials. The president knew that the United States already possessed an excess in nuclear weapons. America could afford to reduce its atomic stockpile by two or three times the amounts that the Russians might contribute to the United Nations agency, and still have an abundant supply of missiles.

THE NUCLEAR THREAT

Even as the nation was busy building a nuclear arsenal, it was also busy trying to figure out how to survive a nuclear attack. During the 1950s and 1960s the American people were in the grip of a civil defense fever—the false idea that surviving a nuclear attack was a simple matter of preparation. Americans were trained to "duck and cover" as the bombs fell. Schoolchildren performed drills where at the sound of an alarm they hid under their wooden desks for protection. It was a pointless exercise.

There was money to be made in preparing for nuclear war. Americans bought fallout shelters and installed them in basements and backyards. Magazines featured advice, recipes, and ideas for entertaining the kids during the nuclear winter. Stores sold freeze-dried foods, flashlights, first-aid kits, and battery-operated radios to stock the home shelters.

Communities built fallout shelters in the basements of public buildings, in subway tunnels, and in other underground spaces. Major corporations constructed fallout shelters for their employees. In 1962, President Kennedy called for "a fallout shelter for everyone."

By the mid-1960s, there were more than 300,000 fallout shelters in American communities, stocked with stale crackers and old bottled water. This effort at preparedness created the illusion of control. It promoted the myth that people could survive a nuclear blast by hiding out in a steel box below the ground.

Government officials knew these efforts were fruitless. Back in 1956, Eisenhower had appointed a retired air force general to work with his staff to calculate the damage that would occur in the initial stages of nuclear war between Russia and the United States. He was presented with two scenarios:

In the first, the attack came without warning until the bombs crossed the early radar warning line. The damage resulted in complete economic collapse for six months to a year; 65 percent of the population needed medical care, but most were unable to receive it.

In the second scenario, there was a month of strategic warning, but no specific information about when the attack would take place. The outcome was much the same, and the idea that the United States would launch its own secret first-strike attack during the warning month was deemed highly unlikely. In both cases, the loss of American life was devastating.

THE SCIENCE RACE

In the mid-1950s, Americans assumed they were ahead of the Soviet Union in terms of technological development. They took for granted that the United States would lead the way in scientific know-how. That changed when the Soviets launched the world's first artificial satellite in October 1957. This satellite—*Sputnik*—left Americans feeling vulnerable. Disturbingly, it came as a complete surprise to the White House and to Ike's science advisors. If the Soviets had the ability to send a satellite into space, they also had the ability to send a nuclear weapon around the globe to hit the United States.

Ike knew that the United States was in a superior position in terms of nuclear strength, but the idea that the Soviets were ahead in space was a huge blow to American prestige. Was America falling behind? Some called it the worst defeat since Pearl Harbor.

The president was annoyed at the criticism. He hated fearmongering. And he didn't think the Soviets' success in space had anything to do with their nuclear capabilities.

But with the midterm elections approaching, *Sputnik* became a useful campaign topic for Democrats. Massachusetts senator John F. Kennedy, running for reelection in 1958, was already being talked about as a presidential candidate. He spoke often about *Sputnik* and the need for better science education.

Both Republicans and Democrats agreed with the need to strengthen science education. If America was to be prepared to meet the challenges of a new scientific and technological age, the country had to invest more in science and math education. The result was the National Defense Education Act, which Ike signed into law in September 1958. The act allotted up to $1 billion in a four-year effort to improve American education, with a special emphasis on the sciences.

Ike also set up the President's Science Advisory Committee to study the nuclear threat and make recommendations. Its finding, called the Gaither Report, proposed a $30 billion investment in fallout shelters and the production of more missiles—not the path Ike favored. The report was used by Democrats, especially Kennedy, in political campaigns. Kennedy argued that Ike and the Republicans weren't as strong as they should be on nuclear defense.

Eisenhower refused to use fear for political advantage. At his final State of the Union address, delivered just eight days before Kennedy's inauguration, Ike said, "We must not return to the 'crash-program' psychology of the past, when each new feint by the communists was responded to in panic. The 'bomber gap' of several years ago was always a fiction, and the 'missile gap' shows every sign of being the same."

Despite Ike's concern about the way Kennedy used the fear of nuclear war in his campaign, he had no choice but to put his faith in the future president. At his final press conference, a reporter asked Ike if it was true that he and Kennedy had hit if off pretty well.

"Well," said Ike, "I don't know if you could put it that way. But I could see that he was willing to learn."

And Ike was willing to teach. He wanted Kennedy to appreciate the need for balance, not just strength. In his farewell address, Eisenhower said:

Our arms must be mighty, ready for instant action, so that no potential aggressor may be tempted to risk his own destruction. But each proposal must be weighed in light of a broader consideration; the need to maintain balance in and among national programs . . . Good judgment seeks balance and progress; lack of it eventually finds imbalance and frustration.

And, he might have added, the potential for destruction.

THE MILITARY-INDUSTRIAL COMPLEX

The potential for the disastrous rise of
misplaced power exists and will persist.
—From Eisenhower's farewell address

PRESIDENT DWIGHT EISENHOWER THOUGHT it was
bad enough that John F. Kennedy was making false
claims about a missile gap to increase American fears
and win an election. But even before the campaign
he had become increasingly disturbed by the prolifera-
tion of ads hyping missile systems in some of America's
most popular consumer magazines. Boeing, McDon-
nell Douglas, and other military contractors purchased
full-page ads in *Life*, *Newsweek*, *Time*, and other magazines. What could possibly be the point of advertising
to ordinary Americans in this way?

Americans were being swept up in the war economy, influenced by muscular images wrapped in the flag. More, better, and increasingly expensive missiles became symbols of patriotism and military strength. Companies that made money from these sales were often motivated by profits rather than patriotism or what was best for the country. Ike thought these advertisements were nothing more than an attempt to make the case for more weapons and to get the American people to put pressure on Congress.

Eisenhower favored balance. His administration allowed the buildup of a massive nuclear arsenal, but he also recognized the need to support domestic programs. He didn't want America to be concerned only with its firepower. He challenged the nation to balance all of its priorities.

This wasn't a new idea for Ike. He'd addressed the issue in his "Chance for Peace" speech during the first year of his presidency, as well as in his farewell speech. He didn't worry about the strength of our military but the source of its power. He didn't think the military-industrial complex was an organized effort by people with wicked intentions, but he did see it as the natural outcome of a free market economy. Companies that produce high-tech weapons want to sell high-tech weapons. Ike saw it as part of his job as president to assess the needs of the country and to decide how many weapons were needed. These were not decisions that should be made by public opinion or shaped by advertising campaigns. Promoting fear to sell missiles did not make the country more secure.

As he prepared to make his case about the military-industrial complex in his farewell speech, he recognized the delicate relationship between the military and the American public. The United States has always had a civilian military—a relatively small permanent force, plus reserves, which can be called on in times of emergency. The founding fathers were committed to the idea that the military be controlled by a free society governed by the people. Countries where the military was a power base in its own right often became military dictatorships. The United States has always tried to limit and balance power. The commander in chief of the military would be a civilian—the president of the United States—but that person does not have the power to go to war. Congress, not the president, has the power to declare war.

Ike considered himself the guardian of a permanent peace, and yet the military–industrial complex was selling a different vision to America. When consumers opened their favorite magazines to see pictures of a Titan missile, they received a powerful message of military might and were vulnerable to the idea of a missile gap. But this was the wrong message. It promoted fear and the sale of weapons, but it didn't make us any safer—and perhaps less so.

Eisenhower worried that this advertising might allow the munitions industry to inappropriately influence Congress. The military economy wasn't something new. It began in the administration of Franklin Roosevelt, who established the War Production Board in 1942, to bring private companies, such as those in the auto industry, into service to produce war machinery. For example, during World War II, General Motors converted all of its factories from making cars to building trucks, tanks, airplanes, and weapons for the military.

After the war, President Roosevelt made the war industry permanent, and companies like Boeing and General Motors kept their defense divisions operational. When Truman became president, he continued the practice. Before 1950, President Truman's advisors pushed him to increase spending on both nuclear and conventional weapons to protect the nation against a potential Soviet threat. The National Security Council report NCS-68, which outlined a plan for American rearmament, stated that increased spending on weapons would also boost the gross national product.

It wouldn't be easy to convince the American public to increase their taxes to pay for an expensive weapons buildup during peacetime. In 1953, companies began their public relations campaigns to create support for increased spending on defense. They argued that the more we spent on the military, the stronger the domestic economy would be. In other words, military spending was a key to national prosperity.

Ike didn't fall for the argument, but it troubled him how easily members of Congress—and perhaps future presidents—could be persuaded by military and private-industry "experts" who might be more interested in their bottom lines or careers than in a reasonable approach to military policy.

Undue influence—even corruption—was inevitable. It was common for industry representatives to try to seek favor with government officials. Sometimes they crossed a line by sending military leaders on exclusive trips. Other times the inappropriate actions involved promises of jobs or infrastructure that military industries could bring to local communities.

Ike's warnings about the rise of the military-industrial complex would be used—and misused—for decades to come. His words were widely quoted by the anti-war movements of the 1960s and beyond. Too often, Eisenhower's subtle and measured tone was lost in an attempt to make his argument simply black and white. In his remarks, Ike didn't argue that there was too much military spending. Instead, he expressed his concern that the military economy had burrowed into communities across America. Every community that housed a military facility or a manufacturing plant that produced military goods wanted to keep those jobs in their hometowns. They were willing to contact their congressional representatives to let them know they wanted to keep things the way they were. Ike challenged this status quo by examining how the nation could achieve real security in balance with other priorities.

STRENGTH THROUGH BALANCE

The idea of expressing his concerns about the military-industrial complex in his farewell speech did not just come to Ike in his final days. He had been talking about it since the early days of his presidency.

Halfway through his second term, Ike began to plan what he would say about the military-industrial complex in his final address. He wanted to cover three central concerns. The first issue was the influence of private industry over the military. The second involved the revolving door from the military to industry. Many people retired from the military in their forties and immediately became directors of aerospace and other related industries. This tight relationship between the military and private industry could undermine the independence of the military, since someone might allow the prospect of a good job to influence a decision. (This practice continues to be a concern today.) Ike's third concern was the domination of military objectives in the awarding of federal and private grants for scientific research. The massive government spending had a direct impact on the shape of the knowledge industry.

With these ideas in mind, Ike's farewell address was crafted against the backdrop of his own presidency. He came into office not only to end the war in Korea, but also to prevent getting involved in any additional conflicts.

During the 1960 presidential campaign, Kennedy had charged the Eisenhower administration—and by extension Nixon—with a weak foreign policy. Kennedy said: "Mr. Nixon has suggested that if he is elected president of the United States, he will go to Eastern Europe . . . I want to make it clear that if I am elected president of the United States, I am going to Washington, DC."

Ike found Kennedy's words empty, meant to stir the pot rather than strengthen America's hand. He worried that Kennedy might rush carelessly into conflicts and build the war machine, rather than cautiously using America's power. He knew Kennedy planned to increase defense spending, which was already 50 percent of the federal budget.

Eisenhower recognized that the nation was entering a new era. Warfare was becoming a matter of sophisticated weaponry and technologies capable of taking us places we might not want to go. The military that Ike was handing Kennedy wasn't the same one that Eisenhower had known when he first joined the army. Instead of rifles, artillery cannons, and cavalry mounts, a Cold War military needed a supply of high-altitude bombers, spy planes, and radar networks.

How could a nation be militarily strong without becoming beholden to a military-industrial complex? As Ike prepared to leave office, he concluded that nuclear weapons were useless in securing a lasting peace, and so their expansion was indefensible and dangerous.

Eisenhower knew that when making his appeal about the dangers of the military-industrial complex, the audience—the American people—would see him as *General* Eisenhower and trust his judgment.

As the television cameras lit up Ike's face in his final address, Americans did not see the excitement and thrill of the New Frontier; they saw a serious veteran confronting a reality the nation was reluctant to face. "Surely, it is impressive that the old soldier should make this warning the main theme of his farewell address," wrote a prominent newspaper columnist. If it were not an important issue, President Eisenhower—General

Eisenhower—would not have made it the theme of his last official speech to the nation.

The morning after Eisenhower's address, the media didn't write too much about it. Ike felt obligated to speak his mind, but he could not force others to listen. The one person he hoped had heard his words was President-Elect John F. Kennedy.

The Eisenhower boys, the early years. Ike is front right, with Edgar behind him; Arthur is holding baby Roy. *Courtesy of the Eisenhower Library*

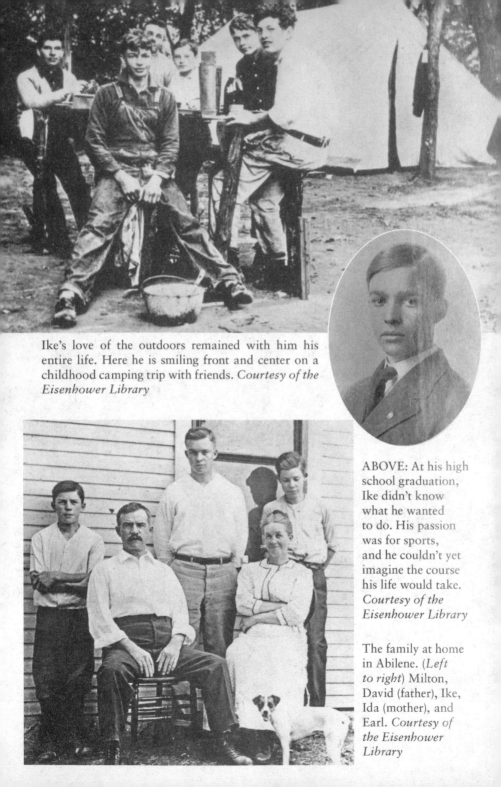

Ike's love of the outdoors remained with him his entire life. Here he is smiling front and center on a childhood camping trip with friends. *Courtesy of the Eisenhower Library*

ABOVE: At his high school graduation, Ike didn't know what he wanted to do. His passion was for sports, and he couldn't yet imagine the course his life would take. *Courtesy of the Eisenhower Library*

The family at home in Abilene. (*Left to right*) Milton, David (father), Ike, Ida (mother), and Earl. *Courtesy of the Eisenhower Library*

Ike's first impression of Mamie was that she was attractive and saucy. She also had a steely will and an endless supply of devotion and support, which she provided during their fifty-three-year marriage. *Courtesy of the Eisenhower Library*

Ike the soldier and commander, as America knew him. He was buried in this uniform. *Courtesy of the Eisenhower Library*

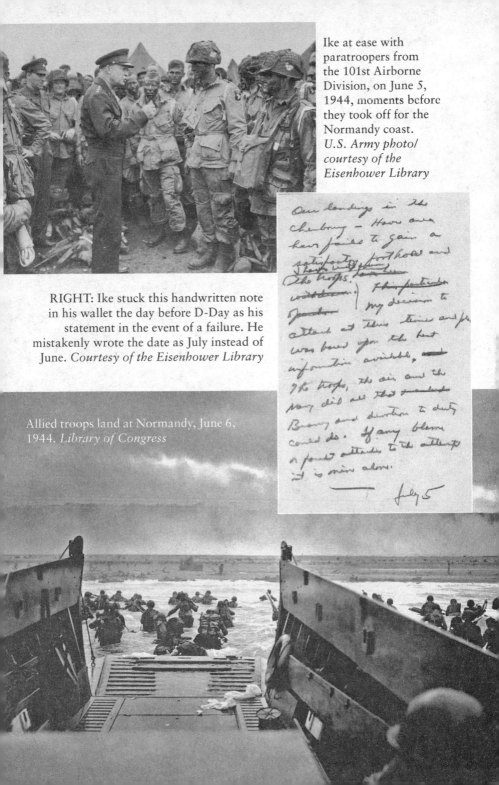

Ike at ease with paratroopers from the 101st Airborne Division, on June 5, 1944, moments before they took off for the Normandy coast. *U.S. Army photo/ courtesy of the Eisenhower Library*

RIGHT: Ike stuck this handwritten note in his wallet the day before D-Day as his statement in the event of a failure. He mistakenly wrote the date as July instead of June. *Courtesy of the Eisenhower Library*

Allied troops land at Normandy, June 6, 1944. *Library of Congress*

"ALL HONOR TO OUR HERO": General Eisenhower returns home. New York City, 1945. *Library of Congress*

"We Like Ike": a once-reluctant candidate on the campaign trail, 1952. *Courtesy of the Eisenhower Library*

Inauguration Day, 1953. Ike took the oath of office on two Bibles—one, a gift from his mother when he graduated from West Point, and the other, the Bible George Washington used to take his oath as the first president. *National Park Service photo/courtesy of the Eisenhower Library*

Cowboy Montie Montana lassos the new president during the inaugural parade, January 20, 1953. *National Park Service photo/courtesy of the Eisenhower Library*

The Castle Bravo nuclear test, March 1954, the largest nuclear detonation at the time. The specter of atomic warfare hung over the Eisenhower years, but Ike navigated the world safely through. *National Nuclear Security Administration*

RIGHT: "President-elect Eisenhower [*left*] during inspection tour at Kimpo [Air Base], Korea," December 1952. Ike made ending the Korean War a priority from the outset, defusing a dangerous flashpoint in the deepening Cold War. *Seymour Johnson AFB Library*

September 25, 1959. When Ike and Khrushchev (*center*) were alone at Camp David, their conversations were warmer than on the public stage. They bonded over a shared love of westerns, but the Cold War tensions remained after the visit. *National Park Service photo/ courtesy of the Eisenhower Library*

Part 3

THE FINAL MISSION

11

GETTING TO KNOW
PRESIDENT-ELECT KENNEDY
JANUARY 18, 1961

DRESSED IN BLACK TIE for a family dinner dance, President-Elect John F. Kennedy had watched on television as President Dwight Eisenhower addressed the nation. No one knows if Kennedy listened intently or casually glanced at the screen while fiddling with his tie. However, there is reason to think the president-elect was paying attention. He was preparing to give the speech of his life—his own inaugural address—three days from then.

Ike's speech was a reply to Kennedy's campaign rhetoric and an advance rebuttal of Kennedy's upcoming inaugural address. Eisenhower probably figured

Kennedy would warn against American weakness in his speech, since that had been a key theme of his campaign. Ike could preempt the attack by highlighting the size and strength of the American military.

After the speech, Kennedy made no public remarks about Eisenhower's address or his reaction to it. He didn't particularly admire Ike, in spite of their polite first meeting on December 6. At least one member of his transition team referred to meetings with Eisenhower as required by protocol rather than helpful.

In most respects Kennedy, a son of privilege, was very different from Ike. He was named for his maternal grandfather, the Boston politician John F. "Honey Fitz" Fitzgerald. In 1946, when Kennedy launched his political career by winning his grandfather's seat in Congress, Ike was already a war hero planning the organization of a peacetime world.

The well-known story about the Kennedys was that the head of the family, Joe Kennedy, intended for his sons to be political giants. During World War II, JFK became a war hero. When a Japanese destroyer sank PT-109, the boat Kennedy was commanding, the young officer saved ten of his men. In recognition of his bravery, Kennedy received the Navy and Marine Corps Medal and a Purple Heart. In June 1944, the *New Yorker* dramatized his story in an article titled "Survival," which was then recirculated in a *Reader's Digest* article. His military career made him well suited for a career in politics.

Kennedy was elected to the House of Representatives and then the Senate. In 1956, Ike was stunned to hear that Senator Kennedy was going to spend more than a million dollars on his reelection campaign. Ike considered it immoral to spend that much money on a political campaign.

A few years later, Kennedy set his sights on the White House. Before the Democratic National Convention in 1960, Speaker of the House Sam Rayburn and Senate Majority Leader Lyndon Johnson dropped in to see Ike. Rayburn said they had to beat Kennedy and make Lyndon president. Johnson, who was a candidate himself, said, "Ike, for the good of the country, you cannot let that man become elected president . . . he's a dangerous man."

Kennedy won the nomination and chose Johnson as his running mate. The Democrats went on to win the election, and Ike sent them a one-sentence message of congratulations after their victory.

With Kennedy as president-elect, Eisenhower feared that everything he'd worked so hard to achieve would be overturned. He worried that the New Frontier would be a wasteland. He saw the transition from his administration to the next as his final chance to put his stamp on Kennedy's term. Ike wanted to influence the young president as much as possible and to allow for a smooth and orderly transition from one administration to the next.

It wasn't easy. Kennedy and his representatives had a heady confidence—a sense of *we've got this*. Ike found this attitude and the media's admiration of Kennedy irritating. He wanted to make sure that Kennedy and his advisors felt the full weight of the deeply complex and troubling issues on the table. For the most part, Kennedy dismissed Ike as a passive president who had created a vast bureaucracy.

During the campaign, Kennedy portrayed Ike as an out-of-touch chief executive whose best days were spent on the golf course. In addition, he was perplexed by Eisenhower's large team of advisors, especially in national security. Kennedy considered himself a forceful leader, who needed the support of only a small group of people closest to him. That included members of his family. Kennedy's most surprising and controversial appointment would be the choice of his brother and campaign manager, Robert, only thirty-five, as attorney general. Many criticized the choice, arguing that the attorney general should have independence from the White House. Ike was bothered by the youth of the new administration. "One of my biggest concerns is that government be run by wisdom instead of by callow youth," Eisenhower said.

When people confronted the new president about his pick for attorney general, JFK disarmed them with a joke. "You know there are a number of people who have complained bitterly about my appointment of Bobby, my brother, as attorney general," he said. "But I just tell them. I say, 'Friend, he's got to get experience someplace.'"

A PEACEFUL HANDOVER

Ike did his best to prepare for the incoming administration. He believed the peaceful handover of power was a signature achievement of democracy.

But it wasn't always easy. When Ike took office, there hadn't been a presidential transition for twenty years, so the process was rusty. (Franklin Roosevelt had been elected to four terms, and Harry Truman took over when he died and then was elected to another term.) Ike also felt that the transfer of power was particularly high stakes in the nuclear age. In addition to managing the awesome power of nuclear weapons, the president had to use strategy and diplomacy to manage America's might around the world.

A presidential transition depended on the goodwill of both sides, often from different political parties. Ike thought about President Truman, who had no transition at all; he had been vice president less than three months when Roosevelt died. He had to be ready from the moment he took office. In fact, he approved dropping atom bombs on Hiroshima and Nagasaki within four months of taking office. In other words, the nuclear age was launched by a man with almost no experience in the Oval Office.

Ike had a difficult transition when he was elected in 1952. During the presidential campaign, Eisenhower and Truman traded slights and betrayals that damaged their relationship. Truman's political partisanship, added to Ike's dislike of political gamesmanship, created a mutual mistrust that lasted throughout the transition period.

The two men's first and only transition meeting, on November 18, 1952, was surrounded with fanfare, orchestrated by Truman. Eisenhower landed in Washington to crowds lining the roads, including government workers given the day off by Truman for the occasion. But when Truman greeted Ike at the White House, the meeting was testy. Ike assumed the show was designed to humiliate him.

Ike believed that Truman had not been acting in America's best interest during his presidency. He felt the nation's international prestige had been damaged by "numerous instances of malfeasance in office, disrespect

for fiscal responsibility, apparent governmental ignorance or apathy about the penetration of Communists
in government, and a willingness to divide industrial
America against itself." Truman took the criticism personally and couldn't rise above it and give Eisenhower
much support as he prepared to take office.

Now that it was his turn to welcome a new president,
Ike realized that the incoming administration would
benefit from a more orderly and in-depth briefing. If he
had his way, Ike would have had the inauguration earlier than January. He thought it was silly that the sitting
president had to go before Congress to give a State of the
Union address just a few days before the new president
took office. His own final State of the Union address
on January 12 was not delivered personally but was read
into the record by the House clerk. It didn't seem to
matter when the nation was focused on the incoming
president.

In addition, it seemed ridiculous for the sitting president to send a budget to Congress. As required, on
January 16 Ike sent his final budget to Congress, and
the Senate majority leader said, "Very interesting. Now
we'll wait and see what the real budget looks like." The
new president would be taking office four days later.

As president, Ike used the organizational skills he had
learned in the military. He developed systems to help

him get things done. He had great respect for the structure of leadership and the coordination of agencies; he saw them as the spokes of a giant wheel of power. He tried to impress these ideas on the president-elect, aware that Kennedy's team thought he was an old fogey.

While some people joked about Ike's use of structural diagrams and administrative details, he had learned through experience that these systems worked. A disorganized mind or a shoot-from-the-hip style of leadership wouldn't work with the complexities of the modern presidency. Ike's White House was a well-run, disciplined shop.

A FINAL PRESS CONFERENCE

On January 18, the day after his farewell address, Ike held his final press conference. He had appeared before reporters 193 times, but the press never seemed to "get" him. Eisenhower wasn't politically driven; he wasn't interested in personalities and gossip. Some in the press thought the president was distant and removed.

Unlike most politicians, Ike didn't try to get all the publicity possible. His lack of connection with the press probably resulted in Ike being underestimated and rarely getting the credit he deserved for his boldest moves.

On the day of his final meeting with reporters as president, Ike was smiling and confident. "I came this morning not with any particularly brilliant ideas about the future," he said, "but I did want the opportunity to say goodbye to people that I have been associated with now for eight years, mostly, I think, on a friendly basis." He smiled and the reporters laughed.

Of course, the press wanted Ike to give his impression of Kennedy. "Well, now, you know, that's the last thing I would do," he said. He did add that he thought the transition was going "splendidly."

When asked about his accomplishments, Ike proudly noted that the nation had been kept at peace during a difficult eight years of the Cold War. America's enemies had developed strong missile programs and there were ongoing threats from the Chinese and the Soviet Union, but America's consistent show of resolve and strength had prevented the worst from happening.

A poignant moment came when Ike was asked what kind of a United States he would like his grandchildren to live in. "I'd say in a peaceful world and enjoying all of the privileges and carrying forward all of the responsibilities envisioned for the good citizens of the United States, and this means among other things the effort always to raise the standards of our people in their spiritual, their intellectual, their economic strength . . ."

When he was done, the reporters, who often had a difficult relationship with Ike, gave him a standing ovation as he left the room.

THE DAY BEFORE
JANUARY 19, 1961

THE MORNING OF HIS last full day in office, President Dwight Eisenhower sat at his desk and wrote a letter to Richard Nixon. He wanted to soothe his vice president, who had been defeated by John F. Kennedy in the presidential election. Nixon had been mocked in defeat, including a brutal joke from Kennedy: "If I've done nothing else for this country, I've saved them from Dick Nixon."

In his letter, Ike also wanted to point a way to the future. Nixon, who had turned forty-eight ten days earlier, was a young man with a political career ahead of him, if he wanted it. Ike might also have been offering an unspoken apology for an embarrassing moment during the campaign. Ike had been asked at a press conference if he could name a major idea of Nixon's he had adopted as president. Caught off guard, Ike said, "If you give me a week, I might think of one. I don't remember." Ike later said he was joking; he didn't mean the remark as a slam against Nixon or his service as vice president. But the press ran with it, raising questions about Nixon's competence at a critical point in the campaign.

In the end, Nixon probably lost the election because of his personality as much as anything. As Eisenhower's personal secretary, Ann Whitman, wrote in her diary, remarking on the difference between her boss and Nixon, "The President is a man of integrity and sincere in his every action . . . He radiates this, everybody knows it, everybody trusts and loves him. But the Vice President sometimes seems like a man who is acting like a nice man rather than being one."

Still, Ike wanted to support and encourage his vice president. In the letter, Ike urged Nixon to press on: "The passage of years has taken me out, so far as active participation is concerned, but the future can still bring to you a real culmination in your service to the country."

Ike had to acknowledge that Nixon had been gracious and pitch-perfect in accepting defeat. In his role as president of the Senate, he had to preside over the Electoral College roll call that formalized his defeat. Instead of suffering through this difficult moment, Nixon turned it around. "This is the first time in one hundred years that a candidate for the presidency announced the result of an election in which he was defeated," Nixon said. "I do not think we could have a more striking and eloquent example of the stability of our constitutional system." His attitude won him a great deal of praise and respect.

After finishing the letter, Ike turned to his final meeting with Kennedy, which was scheduled for nine that morning. It was Ike's last chance to talk at length about the most pressing matters Kennedy would face in only one day's time. Unlike the December 6 meeting, which was introductory in nature, Ike planned for this to be a more strenuous—and even dramatic—meeting.

As they met privately in the Oval Office, Ike decided to show JFK exactly how much power was at his fingertips. A president has to know what to do in the worst-case scenario of a nuclear attack, he told Kennedy. Then he pointed to an officer sitting outside the door, carrying a bag containing nuclear codes and a method for the president to instantly communicate with the Strategic Air Command.

Would Kennedy like to see an example of the power

a president had at hand if he had to rapidly leave the White House? Kennedy smiled and said yes. Ike reached over, pressed a button, and said, "Opal Drill Three." Six minutes later, a helicopter landed on the lawn outside the Oval Office, ready to take the president away.

Kennedy seemed to enjoy the display, although some of his aides later joked about it. Ike's point was that only so much could be communicated with words; sometimes you had to see power with your own eyes.

The conversation that day was sober and thoughtful. "Neither of us apparently felt any impulse to minimize the significance of the transfer of immense responsibilities, now only hours away," Ike later wrote. He enjoyed the intimacy of these one-on-one meetings. Eyeball to eyeball, he hoped to draw Kennedy into a deeper discussion. He found the president elect to be a quick learner, with a sharp mind and a willingness to study. Ike observed that Kennedy had a "hidden hand" too. In their talks, the president-elect was always polite and deferential, but Ike wasn't ever sure what Kennedy actually thought.

After forty-five minutes of private conversation, they walked together into the Cabinet Room to join the larger meeting, including the outgoing and incoming secretaries of state, defense, and treasury, among others.

Ike first focused on global affairs. After all, world

events did not wait for a new president to settle into the job. Eisenhower began by asking the secretary of state to speak about the existing crisis in Laos and Vietnam. There was a real risk that Laos might fall to the communists. The secretary said the Soviets were making trouble in the area, testing Western resolve.

Kennedy listened to the discussion and came away from the meeting feeling that Ike supported military action if it was necessary to stave off the communists. In later years both Kennedy and Lyndon Johnson would claim that Ike approved of military intervention in the area. While it was true that Ike said, "We cannot let Laos fall to the Communists even if we have to fight—with our allies or without them," he added one giant statement that his successors ignored: "It's my conviction that if we ever have to resort to force, there's just one thing to do: clear up the problem completely," Eisenhower said. "We should not allow a situation to develop, costly in both blood and treasure, without achieving our objective."

The most immediate crisis they discussed that day was one taking place only ninety miles off America's shores. On New Year's Day 1959, the revolutionary guerrilla leader Fidel Castro had toppled the corrupt Cuban dictatorship of Fulgencio Batista, driving Batista out of the country. At first the United States was hopeful for a positive change, since Castro's early statements indicated he was willing to establish an elected presidency, and many Latin American nations were lining up in support of the new leader. Then Castro's forces began to murder Batista's loyalists, and by March the State Department reported that communists were influencing the Cuban military and government.

Ike was appalled when the American Society of Newspaper Editors invited Castro to speak in Washington in April. Ike refused to meet him personally, deliberately planning a golf trip. He put Secretary of State Christian Herter, who had stepped into the role after John Foster Dulles resigned in ill health, in charge. He also sent Nixon in his stead. Castro arrived in all his guerrilla glory, with army uniform and boots and a bushy beard, delighting the media as he chowed down on hot dogs, kissed babies, and charmed the country. His charisma created a headache for the administration, which was well aware of Castro's ruthlessness. Notwithstanding Castro's personal appeal, Herter was struck by how naive Castro was: he "was very much like a child in many ways, quite immature regarding problems of government." Nixon's account of the meeting strengthened the fear Castro would be a more vicious dictator than Batista. Nixon challenged him, asking, "Before you came to power you indicated that within a reasonable time there would be elections. When will elections be held?"

"The Cuban people have no faith in elections," Castro said. "They want me. They want Fidel Castro, and I'm going to run the country."

Although he claimed not to be a communist, Castro welcomed the support of communists in the region. Throughout 1960, Castro took over American-owned properties on the island, nationalized refineries, and made it impossible for the United States to continue doing business there. In October, Ike placed an embargo on exports to Cuba. Castro responded by working more closely with the Soviet Union. By January, the United States had broken off diplomatic relations with Cuba, which was now a ticking time bomb off American shores.

Ike understood that Cuba was a tricky problem because Castro was viewed as a hero throughout Latin America. Ike wrote, "They saw him as a champion of the downtrodden and the enemy of the privileged who, in most of their countries, controlled both wealth and governments. His crimes and wrongdoings that so repelled the more informed peoples of the continent had little effect on the young, the peons, the underprivileged, and all others who wanted to see the example of revolution followed in their own nations." Ike called Castro "a little Hitler" and warned against underestimating him.

Castro was an important target during Kennedy's

presidential campaign. Kennedy criticized Nixon: "If you can't stand up to Castro, how can you be expected to stand up to Khrushchev?" What Nixon could not say was that the United States was taking action. Americans were secretly training Cuban exiles in Guatemala, getting them ready for a possible operation against Cuba.

Now that Kennedy had won the election and was preparing to take the presidency, Ike explained the situation. The Cuban exiles were being trained by the Central Intelligence Agency and an assault was in the early planning stages. Ike warned that the forces were not ready to go and certain conditions would have to be met for the effort to be successful. There needed to be a new government ready to take over, including a leader who could replace Castro and Batista. At that point, no such leader had been found.

Ike stressed that the United States was not obligated to follow through with the plan. He saw the plan as one option, and not necessarily the best one. Unfortunately, Kennedy and his advisors heard a different message during the meeting, and this breakdown in communication had disastrous consequences. Kennedy's team would later say they had the impression Ike was urging them to go ahead, when actually he was encouraging them to be cautious. It should be noted that Eisenhower and his senior aides insisted Ike was always extremely careful and precise in his remarks.

During his meeting with Kennedy, Ike felt he'd done the best he could to share his wisdom and offer a model for how the new administration might begin. As he rose to leave, Kennedy shook Ike's hand. "Thank you for giving us everything we asked for, and even quite a few things we haven't, because we didn't know how to ask for them," the president-elect said with a smile. Ike acknowledged that it was impossible to fully prepare for the nature of White House life.

Eisenhower knew he was handing over the presidency in a time of extreme complexity on the world stage to a man with little direct experience of global issues. Cold War tensions had heightened. The situations in Laos, Cuba, and Berlin could break down to put the United States, the Soviet Union, and China on war footing—and that could mean nuclear war. Ike keenly felt that the security of the nation was in greater jeopardy than it had been in the pre-atomic age. Hotheaded, unpredictable people like Castro and inconsistent, secretive leaders like Khrushchev could not be handled with tough talk, and they could not be ignored. Kennedy's words may have worked on the campaign trail, but he now needed to master the more difficult work of diplomacy and intelligence.

When he ran for president, Ike had had the benefit of

understanding the seriousness of these negotiations; he had done them all before—during and after the war. As president, he built a layered fail-safe of advisors, much as he had in the war when each option debated literally had life-and-death consequences. Presidential decisions were often more nuanced than they were in wartime, but he trusted his system to steer him in the right direction. During his meetings with Kennedy he took pains to urge the president-elect to keep the structure in place. It had immeasurable value. Kennedy nodded and smiled, but it wasn't his way and he had no intention of doing it.

LAST NIGHT IN THE WHITE HOUSE

Kennedy left the White House as snow flurries began. He spent a busy afternoon attending receptions, followed by a private conference with President Harry Truman, who had arrived for the inauguration. That night, John and Jackie Kennedy attended a spectacular gala at the National Guard Armory hosted by singer Frank Sinatra and actor Peter Lawford, JFK's brother-in-law. Jackie was luminous in a white ivory silk gown. She looked like a princess against the snowy backdrop.

Among the highlights of the evening was a performance by Sinatra of "That Old Black Magic," changing the words to "That Old Jack Magic." The festivities went on long into the night. While Jackie bowed out early, the president-elect did not arrive home until three in the morning, giving him less than four hours sleep before the most important day of his life.

The snow kept falling until eight inches buried the nation's capital. Throughout the night, 3,000 men and 700 plows tackled the massive effort to clear the snow in preparation for the inaugural festivities.

Back at the White House, many of the staff were forced to usher out Eisenhower's presidency in an unexpected way. Snowed in and unable to go home that final night, they hunkered down in the bomb shelter in the basement of the East Wing. They took advantage of being stranded to hold a farewell party late into the night, while the president and his family were asleep in their beds upstairs.

Ike usually had no trouble going to sleep, a soldier's habit. But sometimes he would wake up after a few hours of sleep and get lost in thought. As drifts of snow blanketed the White House, Eisenhower may have taken a moment to consider the significance of his last hours as president. He may have thought back to President Washington, who completed the nation's first transition of power on March 4, 1797. In that time, leadership of nations usually passed only after death or bloodshed, but Washington wanted to show the world another way. After John Adams took the oath of office in Philadelphia's Congress Hall, the two men prepared to walk out of the room. Adams stepped aside to allow Washington to go first through the door. Washington waited, gesturing Adams to go first. After all, Adams was the president now, and Washington was a private citizen. From that moment forward, the peaceful passing of power was a settled matter in the United States.

On the morning of January 20, 1961, the ritual would be performed once again.

13

THE PASSAGE
JANUARY 20, 1961

PRESIDENT DWIGHT EISENHOWER WOKE at his usual time, 6:15 a.m. The snow had stopped falling overnight and the day was clear, with an icy wind. From the White House he could hear the distant roar of snowplows and trucks removing more than a thousand stalled vehicles from around the capital.

He was at his desk early, wrapping up the final business of his presidency. Most of the farewells had been said. The people who worked in the White House—ushers, housekeepers, police officers, gardeners, cooks, waiters, Secret Service men, and others—had become like family, and it was hard for Ike and Mamie to say goodbye to them. Many of them would stay on and work for the Kennedys. He also said his final goodbyes to the White House staff who had served him so well. Most of them were tearful. Some had hoped to have a role in a Nixon White House, which was not to be.

Shortly after eleven, John and Jackie Kennedy arrived at the North Portico, and Ike strode out to meet them, coatless and hatless, ushering them into the warm interior like a perfect host. Minutes later the Johnsons drove up, and once again Ike went outside to bring them inside. Coffee was served in the first-floor state reception room, called the Red Room for its red upholstery, wallpaper, and draperies. The conversation was friendly and high-spirited. Sitting next to Jackie on a settee, John Eisenhower told her how much she would love the house and how wonderful the staff was. She smiled politely, but he could tell her thoughts were elsewhere.

Ike did make one concession to tradition and to Kennedy's style. Although Ike had enraged Truman by not wearing a stovepipe hat to his inauguration in 1953, he wore one now to match Kennedy's.

At the Capitol, seated between Eisenhower and Johnson, Kennedy made small talk with Ike in a friendly manner before the ceremony began. There were various delays due to the weather. Washington was still recovering from the snowstorm. National Airport was closed, and former president Herbert Hoover was among the thousands who found their planes turned back, so he missed the inauguration. Despite the cold, one million people lined the streets to watch the inaugural parade.

As soon as the ceremony began, there was another problem. As Cardinal Cushing of Boston began his invocation, smoke began pouring out of the lectern. Cushing's immediate thought was that it might be a bomb, but it was only a short circuit in the wiring. To break the tension, Ike leaned over and murmured to Kennedy, "You must have a hot speech."

Once the ceremony was under way, Marian Anderson sang the national anthem and Robert Frost took the microphone to read a poem he had written for the occasion. The eighty-three-year-old Frost was frail and shaking, and after struggling to read the poem in the glare of a blazing winter sun, he gave up and recited another poem, "The Gift Outright," which he knew by heart. Johnson and Kennedy took their oaths of office, and at last it was time for Kennedy's speech.

Kennedy draped his coat over his chair and removed his stovepipe hat, despite the cold. He appeared to Americans watching on TV as especially youthful and vigorous. (He was wearing long underwear.) JFK's inaugural address, brief and powerful, was a masterful blend of poetry and ideology—a stunning performance still regarded as one of the best speeches in our nation's history.

Many who heard Kennedy's speech questioned if he wrote it himself. Ike never hid the fact that he had speechwriters—but he worked with them to make the words his own. Most people understood and accepted that presidents didn't have time to write all of their speeches without assistance.

Although people around JFK knew—and history would record—that Theodore Sorensen played a key role in preparing Kennedy's address, there was an attempt to claim that the new president had written the speech entirely on his own. Before his death in 2010 Sorensen acknowledged he had destroyed an early draft of the speech, which he had written by hand, at the request of Jacqueline Kennedy, who wanted her husband to be given sole credit for writing it.

Over the years Sorensen was often pressed to say whether or not he had written the famous line "Ask not what your country can do for you, ask what you can do for your country." Later in his career, he addressed this issue this way: "Having no satisfactory answer, I long ago started answering the oft-repeated question as to its authorship with the smiling retort: 'Ask not.'"

It should be noted that the people asked to make great

speeches are those who have the least time to work on their prose. Ike, who did try to work on many of his speeches during his presidency, also acknowledged that speechmaking was a big job. "The president of the United States, naturally, must be ready at an instant's notice to address himself fluently on any topic from the largest pumpkin ever grown—just that moment presented to him—to the State of the Union and the world," he said after he left office.

Kennedy also had a strong hand in his speeches, especially this one. He was known to be an eloquent speaker, and he favored soaring rhetoric over simple words.

Edward R. Murrow devoted his final newscast, on January 22, 1961, to a comparison of Ike's farewell address with Kennedy's inaugural address. Eisenhower, he said, focused on the impact of the world situation on our society: "The Eisenhower concern, as I read it, was a fear that we may lose our liberties while preparing to defend them." Of the military-industrial complex, Murrow observed that Ike was speaking back to Kennedy's claims in the campaign that our nation was growing weaker. Instead, Murrow said, Eisenhower "was, in fact, suggesting that the machine may get beyond human or political control, that we could reach a point where, in fact, 'things would be in the saddle and ride mankind.'"

In contrast, Kennedy's speech was muscular, even defiant. Some even suggested that the line "we shall pay any price, bear any burden, meet any hardship, support any friend, oppose any foe" was perhaps more forceful than necessary.

While sitting on the platform during the inauguration, Ike thought that the stage where he was sitting was a perfect target for an enemy that wanted to attack the mechanism of government. After all, almost every political leader of national significance was gathered there. He also realized that the next twenty-four hours—Kennedy's first day in office—was equally dangerous. If an emergency were to occur, a brand-new president might not be ready to respond effectively. Ike was glad he'd done all he could to prepare Kennedy for what he might face.

HOME TO PRIVATE LIFE

As the inauguration concluded, Ike shook Kennedy's hand vigorously, feeling the weight of eight years fall away. Making his way to a side entrance, his arm around Mamie, Ike realized that for the first time in their married life, they were private citizens, serving neither the military nor the government.

Ike and Mamie walked alone to their car, which would take them to a private luncheon hosted by the former chairman of the U.S. Atomic Energy Commission. By midafternoon, the Eisenhowers were heading home, traveling the eighty-five miles to Gettysburg in the family car, a 1955 Chrysler Imperial. It was driven by John Moaney, who had served as Ike's personal assistant since World War II. Moaney, an African American army sergeant, and his wife, Delores, became indispensable to the Eisenhowers. During Ike's retirement, Moaney would continue his service, and then stay on with Mamie after Ike died. In some respects, Moaney was closer to Ike than any human being apart from Mamie.

As they crossed the snowy landscape on their way to Pennsylvania, Ike and Mamie marveled at the life they had lived, noting that they had stayed at the White House longer than any other place during their forty-four years of marriage. They were touched to see crowds lining the roads, bundled against the cold, to cheer their return to Gettysburg. The crowds grew larger as they neared the farm. People waved flags and shouted "God bless you" and "We love you."

That evening the family gathered for dinner at John and his wife Barbara's house. Before eating, John offered a toast to his father: "Leaving the White House will not be easy at first, but we are reunited as a family, and this is what we have wanted," John said. "I suppose that tonight we welcome back a member of this clan who has done us proud."

Everyone, including Ike, raised their glasses and shouted, "Hear! Hear!" For the first time during that week of change and transition, Ike fought back tears.

The next day, Ike received a warm note from President Kennedy:

> *My dear Mr. President*
>
> *On my first day in office I want to send you a note of special thanks for your many acts of cordiality and assistance during the weeks since the election.*
>
> *I am certain that your generous assistance has made this one of the most effective transitions in the history of our Republic. I have very much enjoyed personally the associations which we have had in this common effort.*
>
> *With all good wishes to you and Mrs. Eisenhower in the days ahead, I am*
>
> *Sincerely,*
>
> *John F. Kennedy*

Ike was pleased to receive Kennedy's gracious note, and he could only hope the new president was ready for the job. The transition can make or break a new president's first days. In spite of what he considered meaningful personal conversations with Kennedy, Ike admitted to himself that he had no idea what impact—if any—his words had on the new president.

Private life was an entirely new experience for Ike. During much of his military career and then as president, Ike had staff to meet most of his basic needs. Right away he ran into trouble. On his first day home, he came out of his office looking for the Secret Service agent who had been assigned to him for thirty days. "There's something wrong with the telephone," he said. "I keep trying to dial this number, and I keep getting wrong numbers or getting the operator."

The agent checked the phone and it worked fine. It turned out that Ike had been dialing the phone wrong; he was rotating the dial as if it were a safe combination. The Secret Service agent taught the former president how to dial a telephone, and the problem was solved.

Ike was also rusty when it came to driving a car. The owner of the Gettysburg Hotel, where Ike and Mamie sometimes dined, admitted that when the president had a reservation, he made sure all the parked cars were removed from the front of the hotel to give the former president plenty of room to get around.

There was a long list of things Ike hadn't done in thirty years, if ever. He'd never been in a drugstore or supermarket, never shopped for clothing, never been to a barbershop. He didn't know what a drive-in movie was or a Laundromat. When an article came out describing him as out of touch, Mamie was offended, but Ike said, "I don't see what's wrong with it. It's all true."

Ike didn't mind learning about civilian life, but he did have one special request. Having served eight years at the will of the people, what Ike wanted most was to return to the man he was—the soldier. To that end, he asked Kennedy to have Congress restore his status as a five-star general. He was willing to give up the title "Mr. President" if this could be done.

Kennedy didn't understand the request. He couldn't imagine why Ike would rather be called "General Eisenhower" than "Mr. President," a titled earned by so few. Before he left office, Ike drafted a bill for Congress, and when Kennedy presented it, it easily passed. On March 24, 1961, Kennedy signed into law the commission restoring the rank of five-star general of the army to Eisenhower. The following day the army's five-star pennant was raised on the flagpole at Ike's Gettysburg farm.

KENNEDY STARTS HIS PRESIDENCY

On January 30, 1961, Kennedy delivered his own State of the Union speech, only eighteen days after Eisenhower's. Ike was on a hunting vacation in Georgia and didn't see or hear the address, which was probably for the best. Although Ike's State of the Union was generally optimistic, Kennedy's was a harsh warning about the state of the economy, an "hour of peril," as he described it.

While Ike was reinventing himself at Gettysburg, Kennedy was making his own mark on the White House. Unfortunately, one of the first things he did was to dismantle the safety systems that had served Eisenhower so well. The national security advisor quickly did away with Eisenhower's system of committees and broad input for decision making. Kennedy relied on a very streamlined National Security Council staff.

Kennedy's team reacted to Eisenhower's super-organized way of governing by becoming too anti-organizational, letting it be known that the new president would chart his own course. Kennedy preferred a one-man show.

In part because of his lack of organization and his unwillingness to hear differing points of view, Kennedy made some serious mistakes while in office. He spent a great deal of time on crisis management rather than carrying out his vision, according to some historians. Kennedy's first challenge would come less than three months into his term. It was, among other things, a failure created by the lack of an organized system of advisors. As Ike would write in *Mandate for Change*, "Organization cannot make a genius out of an incompetent . . . On the other hand, disorganization can scarcely fail to result in inefficiency and can easily lead to disaster."

14

A SPRING DAY AT CAMP DAVID
APRIL 22, 1961

AS GENERAL DWIGHT EISENHOWER'S helicopter came into view over the treetops of Camp David, President John F. Kennedy stood near the helipad to greet him. The commander in chief had sent the helicopter for Eisenhower, who came in from his farm in Gettysburg to offer advice to the man who had moved into the White House just three months earlier. Kennedy needed help as he faced a catastrophe that threatened to ruin his presidency.

Eisenhower greeted Kennedy warmly, and the two men strolled along the tree-lined paths. This was Kennedy's first visit to Camp David, and Ike was in the position of showing the president the grounds.

Kennedy aide David Powers, who a few months earlier dismissed Eisenhower as outdated and unimportant to the new administration, had a new appreciation of what Ike could teach the young president. "When I saw them together that day . . . I was thinking of President Kennedy, the youngest man ever elected at the age of forty-three, and President Eisenhower, the oldest man up to that time ever elected president of the United States," Powers said. "And as I watched them I was thinking of the advice that President Kennedy was going to receive that day, not from President Eisenhower, from General Eisenhower, the old warrior."

As Eisenhower and Kennedy walked together, they discussed world events and shared the heavy hearts of two men burdened by the weight that only a president can feel. The central topic of conversation—and the reason Kennedy brought Ike to Camp David—was the Bay of Pigs invasion, which had started five days earlier.

By almost every account, including Kennedy's own, the Bay of Pigs disaster was a fatal combination of mixed signals, poor planning, and a last-minute decision to withdraw air support for the mission. Back in January, during their last meeting, Ike told Kennedy that Castro needed to be dealt with, but he wasn't sure how. Ike had started to develop a plan for an invasion of Cuba, but the idea had not been fully developed. The mission would be carried out under Kennedy's administration, so he had to decide how he wanted to handle the problem.

When Kennedy became president, he received conflicting input about carrying out the Cuban invasion. The Central Intelligence Agency urged the president to launch the invasion. Other advisors told him to wait. Kennedy and his national security advisors decided to move forward, and they didn't want to hear dissenting opinions. As a result, the voices of caution remained unheard. "For God's sake be careful," warned National Security Council foreign policy officer Samuel E. Belk. "Be sure that the military and CIA are telling you the truth." His words went unheeded.

The experts who understood the invasion plan argued that American air support was needed for victory. Kennedy wasn't sure about that. He told the CIA he didn't want the invasion to be seen as an "American" program, which it clearly would be if the military took part in an air assault. It's unclear how Kennedy thought the invasion could succeed without it.

Without confidence about the mission, Kennedy ordered that the plan move forward. Shortly after midnight on April 17, 1961, some 1,400 Cuban exiles landed on the coast of southern Cuba in an area known as the Bay of Pigs. Castro had learned in advance about the "secret" mission, so he was ready for the invaders when they landed in Cuba. Kennedy personally canceled the air cover for the operation, still worried about putting an American signature on the effort. His decision to withdraw air support doomed the mission. One hundred and fourteen people were killed and more than twelve hundred more were captured.

The Bay of Pigs was the first test of Kennedy's presidency, and it was a disaster.

One of Kennedy's flaws was his belief that he could act as his own secretary of state, much as former president Franklin Roosevelt had done. Kennedy's secretary of state, Dean Rusk, had been skeptical about the Bay of Pigs plan from the beginning. He didn't think it would work and he thought it violated international law. There was no way to make a good legal case for an American-supported landing in Cuba. There was also no evidence that the Cuban people wanted to overthrow Castro. However, instead of pushing Kennedy to rethink the mission, Rusk said very little.

EISENHOWER COUNSELS KENNEDY

When face-to-face with Eisenhower, Kennedy confessed the Bay of Pigs operation had been a complete failure. Everything had gone wrong—the intelligence, the timing, the tactics. Kennedy worried it could leave a permanent stain on his presidency.

"No one knows how tough this job is until he's been in it a few months," Kennedy said to Ike.

Eisenhower smiled. "Mr. President," he said, "if you will forgive me, I think I mentioned that to you three months ago."

Kennedy smiled back. "I certainly have learned a lot since then."

Ike would later reflect, "he seemed himself at that moment"—no longer the cocky king of the New Frontier, but a man facing the truth.

Eisenhower had not been told about the invasion before it occurred. Now the man who had planned the greatest military operation in world history—D-Day—questioned JFK about his preparations. Who recommended it? What was the nature of the debate? Were there changes in the plan while it was under way?

"Well," said Kennedy, "I just approved a plan that had been recommended by the CIA and by the Joint Chiefs of Staff. I took their advice."

Ike nodded. "Mr. President," he asked, "before you approved this plan, did you have anybody in front of you debating the thing so you got the pros and cons yourself and then made the decision, or did you see these people one at a time?"

"Well, I did have a meeting . . . I just took their advice," the president said.

Kennedy's response troubled Ike. Clearly, the president had not engaged in a vigorous give-and-take, and he might not have fully understood all the consequences of the action he was about to take. Ike's own National Security Council meetings were methodical and thorough, with each person at the table presenting his position, followed by debate. He liked to hear differing points of view to open up his thinking.

"Mr. President, were there any changes in the plan that the Joint Chiefs of Staff had approved?" Ike asked.

Kennedy explained that they called off some of the bombing. "We felt it necessary that we keep our hand concealed in this affair," he said. "We thought that if it was learned that *we* were really doing this rather than the rebels themselves, the Soviets would be apt to cause trouble in Berlin."

Ike was astonished. "Mr. President, how could you expect the world to believe that we had nothing to do with it?" he asked. "Where did those people get the ships to go from Central America to Cuba? Where did they get the weapons? . . . How could you have possibly kept from the world any knowledge that the United States was involved? I believe there is only one thing to do when you get into this kind of thing—it must be a success."

Eisenhower imagined the way the Kennedy

administration would try to twist the story when talking to the media by blaming Ike for the invasion and its failure. Kennedy's people were saying, in effect, Ike told him to do it and he trusted Ike.

This wasn't right. Kennedy had been reluctant to adopt plans and organizational systems from Eisenhower's administration. The plan to train Cuban exiles for an invasion was little more than an idea when Ike left office. Ike had plainly told Kennedy back in January that any kind of mission depended on first finding the organization and leadership able to actually carry out an overthrow of Castro.

Together, Eisenhower and Kennedy faced the press. "I asked President Eisenhower here to bring him up to date on recent events and get the benefit of his thoughts and experience," Kennedy said.

Of course, the reporters were very interested in hearing Ike's verdict, which he would not give them. "I am all in favor of the United States supporting the man who has to carry the responsibility for our foreign affairs," he said. He had not come to Camp David to criticize the president.

Ike returned home, but he continued to worry about what was going on in the White House. His fear that Kennedy would dismantle the National Security Council systems had been realized. Ike had tried during their two meetings to stress the importance of having a strong and well-organized system for the National Security Council, because these discussions could protect a president from making mistakes. The Kennedy administration saw these systems as nothing but red tape that slowed and complicated decision making. Unfortunately, Kennedy's people—and Kennedy himself—had been so eager to cut the red tape that they ended up cutting the safety net instead.

Kennedy was embarrassed and angry. He felt betrayed by the CIA and his military leadership. He fired the head of the CIA and the man who had planned the operation. He also took responsibility for what happened and learned a lot about the need to make careful decisions in the future.

The president also realized that Kennedy's personality played a role in the disaster. He liked to be in charge and make decisions. He didn't like to wait. Being decisive is a good quality for a president, but sometimes it is wiser to wait to receive more guidance before acting.

After the Bay of Pigs invasion, Kennedy was more open about seeking Ike's advice—most of the time. Kennedy ignored another of Ike's warnings, probably to his regret. Back in December 1960, when the two men met for the first time, Kennedy had asked Ike if he thought he should set up a meeting with Soviet leader Nikita

Khrushchev. Ike said he thought the president-elect should wait until his presidency was well established before meeting with the Soviet leader.

Kennedy didn't listen. He arranged for a June 1961 summit with the Soviet leader in Vienna. The meeting didn't go well. One exchange was particularly alarming. "It is up to the U.S. to decide whether there will be war or peace," Khrushchev said at the end of a difficult conversation.

Frustrated, Kennedy snapped back: "Then, Mr. Chairman, there will be war. It will be a cold winter."

The relationship between the United States and the Soviet Union continued to decline, and two months later the Berlin Wall went up.

Looking on, Ike was furious about the Berlin Wall, and deeply worried about Kennedy's openly hostile relationship with Khrushchev. This was no time for drama.

KENNEDY FACES OFF WITH KHRUSHCHEV

The Bay of Pigs fiasco was followed by the Cuban Missile Crisis, one of the worst conflicts of Kennedy's presidency. For the first time, Americans feared that we were actually on the brink of a nuclear attack.

Unknown to Kennedy, when he met with Khrushchev in June, the Soviet leader had already made plans with Castro to place Soviet nuclear-armed missiles in

Cuba. The Soviet Union said these missiles were needed to protect itself from United States aggression. The United States first learned about the plan on October 14, 1961, when a U-2 spy plane flying over Cuba took photos of intermediate-range missile sites being built on the island. These weapons could easily reach the United States. Kennedy was told about the missile sites on October 16, and he informed Congress.

Kennedy's critics in Congress immediately called it a disastrous failure of intelligence, arguing that the missile sites did not just spring up overnight. How did American intelligence miss months of activity? Kennedy wanted to focus on what to do about the situation now.

The Soviet minister of foreign affairs told Kennedy in a White House meeting that the missiles were for defensive purposes only, but the Americans could not let them stay just ninety miles from American shores.

Many of Kennedy's advisors were recommending a direct attack on the missile sites. Others thought the military should invade Cuba. This time Kennedy held back.

In a strong letter to Khrushchev on October 22, 1962, Kennedy wrote, "In our discussion and exchanges on Berlin and other international questions, the one thing that has most concerned me has been the possibility that your Government would not correctly understand the will and determination of the United States in any given situation, since I have not assumed that you or any other sane man would, in this nuclear age, deliberately plunge the world into war which it is crystal clear no country could win and which could only result in catastrophic consequences to the whole world." The president went on to promise Khrushchev that the Americans would do anything in their power to prevent the breach of security posed by missiles in Cuba.

Khrushchev responded that the missiles were for defense, not aggression. He concluded, "I hope that the United States Government will display wisdom and renounce the actions pursued by you, which may lead to catastrophic consequences for world peace."

On October 22, hours before addressing the American people about the crisis, Kennedy called Eisenhower. "What about if the Soviet Union—Khrushchev— announces tomorrow, which I think he will, that if we attack Cuba that it's going to be nuclear war?" Kennedy asked Eisenhower. "And what's your judgment as to the chances they'll fire these things off if we invade Cuba?"

"Oh, I don't believe that they will," Ike said. "Something may make these people [the Soviets] shoot them off. I just don't believe this will . . . I will say this. I'd want to keep my own people very alert."

"Well, we'll hang on tight," Kennedy said.

In his speech to the nation at seven that evening—which he knew would be seen around the world—Kennedy presented the evidence that the Soviets had placed missiles in Cuba, and he called for their removal. He also announced the establishment of a naval blockade around the island until the Soviet Union removed the missile sites and guaranteed that no further missiles would be shipped to Cuba. He followed up with a second letter to Khrushchev, informing him that Soviet ships bound for Cuba would not be allowed through.

Khrushchev responded with rage. "You, Mr. President, are not declaring a quarantine, but rather are setting forth an ultimatum and threatened that if we do not give in to your demands you will use force . . . You are no longer appealing to reason, but wish to intimidate us."

This was the most dangerous moment of the crisis. Castro demanded that the Soviets use nuclear weapons to attack the United States if they invaded Cuba to remove the missile sites. At the same time, Khrushchev remained angry that his ships were stalled in the water, unable to reach Cuba. The situation was explosive.

Eisenhower's assessment of the situation ended up being correct. Khrushchev did not want a nuclear confrontation. He wanted a face-saving compromise that would also protect Cuba from United States aggression.

Kennedy was willing to give him that. In the following three days, both countries worked behind the scenes to come up with a solution. Khrushchev's final demand, which Kennedy felt he could live with, was an agreement to remove the missile sites in exchange for a promise that the United States would not attack Cuba, and also an agreement to remove American missiles that were posted in Turkey. They also agreed that United States officials could conduct inspections to ensure the sites had been removed.

Ike was on the farm, sitting on the porch with a friend, when Kennedy phoned on October 28 to say that a tentative deal had been reached: the missile sites would be removed in exchange for the United States agreeing that it would never invade Cuba.

After Ike listened, he said, "Now the only thing I would suggest, Mr. President, is this. What you say you will do, whether it is an inspection by us, or whatever concessions we are prepared to make, do this very specifically: Make sure it is written down. And then by all means do everything you say you are going to do. Because if you don't do it, pretty soon you will find that you can't possibly do it. Don't sign a blank check."

"We will agree we will not invade Cuba provided there are none of these offensive weapons allowed to stay there," Kennedy said.

But Ike pressed him. "Other conditions might come up," he argued, "when you would have to enter Cuba sometimes, and I think you ought to define the circumstances in which you might go in."

"Well," said Kennedy, "the Soviets are agreeing that we can go on land and make land inspections."

"All right, then. There is one thing you must do. Because if we don't do it, they will say it is because you are weak."

But the land inspections never happened. Castro immediately protested that Khrushchev might have agreed to this but it was, after all, his country. And Kennedy relented—really, he had no other choice without stirring up the aggressions all over again.

A NATION TRAUMATIZED

November 19, 1963, marked the 100th anniversary of Abraham Lincoln's Gettysburg Address, and President Kennedy was asked to speak at the ceremony. He declined, citing a prescheduled political trip to Texas. And so Eisenhower rose to the occasion, giving what for him was an unusually poetic speech. "Lincoln had faith that the ancient drums of Gettysburg, throbbing mutual defiance from the battle lines of the blue and the gray, would one day beat in unison, to summon a people, happily united in peace, to fulfill, generation by generation, a noble destiny," he said. "His faith has been justified—but the unfinished work of which he spoke in 1863 is still unfinished; because of human frailty, it always will be."

Three days after Eisenhower's speech, on November 22, the human frailty he mentioned would be deeply felt when President Kennedy was assassinated in Dallas. The assassination, apparently carried out by lone gunman Lee Harvey Oswald, occurred while the president and first lady rode in an open car motorcade.

Kennedy's death traumatized the nation. The youthful spirit of the president—and the sight of small children romping in the White House—had become a feature of American life that went beyond politics. Some people may not have agreed with Kennedy's politics, but personally he was loved around the world. After his death, the nation went into mourning. Schools closed, churches filled, and Americans spent days in front of their television screens, trying to make sense of what had happened.

The day after the assassination, Ike went to Washington to pay his respects and view the casket, which was lying in state. Afterward, he had lunch with the new president, Lyndon Johnson. "I need you more than ever now," Johnson said. Ike gave him the best advice he could—to be his own man—something that would require enormous patience and skill. Grateful, Johnson asked Ike if he could write a memo with advice for him going forward.

Ike prepared a thoughtful letter for Johnson. Ike had strong political instincts, and he put the good of the nation above party politics. Among his other suggestions, Ike urged Johnson to call a joint session of Congress: "Point out first that you have come to this office unexpectedly and you accept the decision of the Almighty," Eisenhower advised. Then, he wrote, tell Congress it will be your mission to carry out "the noble objectives so often and so eloquently stated by your great predecessor." Johnson's address to Congress, five days after Kennedy's death, followed Ike's script and was both humble and steadfast, winning him an enormous amount of goodwill from the American people.

Kennedy's funeral and burial took place on November 25. President Hoover was too frail to attend, but Truman and Eisenhower were seated together in the same pew in Saint Matthew's Cathedral. By this point, they were old men—Truman seventy-nine and Eisenhower seventy-three—and any disagreements they might have had with the young president no longer seemed important. Johnson, who had once fought to win the seat in the Oval Office, looked haggard and ill that day.

On this solemn occasion, Truman and Eisenhower

gave one another the benefit of the doubt. Before the funeral, Ike asked Truman, who was attending the ceremony with his daughter Margaret, if they would like to ride with him and Mamie in their car, and they agreed. After the service, the Trumans invited the Eisenhowers to stop by and have a sandwich before driving home. Over supper, the two ex-presidents spoke intimately about the experiences they shared. Hours passed as they engaged in meaningful conversation. There was no single moment of reconciliation, but rather a mutual appreciation for how much they had in common.

Ike continued to be a counselor to President Johnson, who proved to be far more willing to seek advice than Kennedy had. Johnson's presidency was shaped by the fighting in Vietnam. As the situation in Vietnam grew worse, Johnson called Ike to the White House again and again, seeking advice more from the general than the ex-president. Ike offered the best advice he could, urging Johnson to overwhelm the enemy with a show of force, something Johnson was never able to do.

There was some misunderstanding about Ike's attitudes toward Vietnam. Johnson often claimed that he was merely continuing the policies started under the Eisenhower and Kennedy administrations. But that wasn't true: Ike didn't support sending troops to Vietnam.

Johnson saw a political advantage in tying his actions

in Vietnam to Ike's policies. Most presidents try to blame their troubles on the challenges they inherited from a previous administration. Under Eisenhower there were 600 soldiers serving in an economic and technical aid program in Vietnam. Under Johnson, there were 500,000 troops engaged in combat. Johnson wanted to be seen as following the same strategy as Ike, but it wasn't the same. Johnson and Kennedy had expanded the war and now Johnson had to figure out a way to win or get out.

At the time, the anti-war protests took to the street to speak out against the fighting. Ike shared Johnson's disappointment in the war protest movement. He felt that the young protesters lacked respect for authority and were unwilling to help protect the freedom they enjoyed. "No one could hate war more than I," Ike wrote to his grandson David. "But I get very upset when I find people who are quite willing to enjoy the privileges and rights afforded by their country but publicly announce their readiness to flout their responsibilities."

Whenever Johnson asked for help, Ike made time for him. In this period of his life, Eisenhower was also very busy with speaking engagements and writing, publishing a two-part presidential memoir, a diary, and a book of personal stories, *At Ease: Stories I Tell to Friends.*

"GOD TAKE ME"

By 1968, Ike's health was failing. He suffered another heart attack in April, and while recovering at Walter Reed Army Medical Center in Washington DC, he followed the Republican primaries. His former vice president, Richard Nixon, was engaged in a heated battle for the nomination. Many people wondered why Ike hadn't endorsed Nixon. Once again, the two men were trapped in the awkwardness that defined their relationship. Nixon refused to ask for an endorsement; he didn't want to be pushy or beg for support. Ike didn't come out in support of Nixon until July 18, just a few weeks before the convention.

Ike wasn't strong enough to make it to the convention, but he prepared a taped statement that was shown to delegates on the first night of the convention. The following day, Ike had another heart attack. When Nixon finally won the Republication presidential nomination, he called on the delegates to "win this one for Ike."

Ike remained at Walter Reed. He lived to see Nixon elected president, and after his inauguration President Nixon stopped by the hospital to visit. In a photo of that occasion, Ike looked thin, but he was grinning widely, delighted with Nixon's success.

During the coming month, Eisenhower became weaker. Two days before he died, he called his brother

Milton to his side. Milton leaned in close to his brother. "I want you to know how much you have always meant to me," Ike said. "How much I have valued your counsel." Milton left the room and broke into tears.

As he neared the end, Ike ordered the blinds closed to shut out the sun. He asked to be lifted up in bed and said, "I want to go. God take me."

Soon after, he lost consciousness.

He died at 12:25 p.m. on March 28, 1969.

The following day, pallbearers carried Ike's coffin inside the National Cathedral in Washington for the first stage of five days of official ceremonies. Ike's body, dressed in his army uniform and resting in the eighty-dollar army-issue casket he had requested, lay in the Bethlehem Chapel for twenty-four hours, as the people filed by to pay their respects.

On the afternoon of March 30, a dramatic processional formed to take the casket to the Capitol, where it would lie in state. Thousands of people lined the streets as the casket was transferred to a horse-drawn caisson, which had originally been used to carry cannons.

Although he had been out of office and away from the limelight for years, in death Ike was remembered as the tireless soldier who had helped to win World War II. His death triggered an emotional outpouring from those who remembered him from that time. As his body lay in state in a flag-draped coffin in the Capitol Rotunda, more than 40,000 Americans lined up in unseasonably cold weather to say goodbye. The people walked quietly past his coffin, averaging as many as 2,000 an hour long into the night and continuing until the afternoon of the second day. Although the Eisenhower family had requested that people donate to charity in lieu of flowers, bouquets poured in. There were so many that five soldiers were assigned to handle the floral arrangements.

On March 31, a majestic funeral procession formed to take Ike back to the National Cathedral for the funeral. After Ike died, Mamie had reached out to Chuck Yeager, the famous brigadier general and test pilot, asking if he could organize a flyby down Pennsylvania Avenue on the day of the funeral.

The skies above Washington were overcast and foggy on March 31, so it looked like a no-go. To Yeager's surprise, he received a call from General John Paul McConnell, the chief of staff of the air force, who was overseeing the funeral activities, asking him to do the flyby.

Yeager led the formation down Pennsylvania Avenue, skirting treetops as the crowds looked to the skies in awe.

After the ceremony, the casket was taken to Union Station for the trip home to Abilene, Kansas, Ike's final resting place. Crowds—including high school bands and children waving American flags—lined the railway stops along the route. On April 2, a final religious service and parade brought Ike to his burial place in a small chapel on the grounds of his presidential library, a few yards from his childhood home.

"The hero has come home," a somber Walter Cronkite told American viewers. "It has been noted more than once these past five days that the nation mourns but does not weep. Today's ceremonies in this midwestern town mark the end of a life, an era, and an age. You may feel regret that the age is past, but there can be no complaints about the quality of the life."

IKE'S POWERFUL LEGACY

Some years after Eisenhower's death, his brother Milton wrote that after all the challenges and conflicts Ike had faced during his presidency, it was too bad he hadn't lived long enough to hear his time in office referred to as "the good old days." It's human nature to look longingly at the past.

Today, over a half a century after Ike delivered his farewell address, the nation is giving the man and his words another look. As America engaged in wars in Afghanistan and Iraq, Ike's final message about military investment became an issue once again. His speech came out of the archives and was examined anew.

Ike's farewell address, delivered three days before the end of his presidency, became one of the most-quoted presidential speeches in history. Still, it's hard to talk about the lessons derived from Ike's military-industrial complex speech without oversimplifying the issues. Eisenhower's words can be heard differently depending on your politics and your feelings about military spending, troop strength, and the role of industry.

For those who oppose war, Ike's words seem to argue that the United States should reduce military spending in favor of support for domestic programs.

For those concerned with fraud and waste in government, Ike's words suggest a military involved in backroom deals and secret agreements between powerful industries and congressional committees. Since the speech has been cited so often by anti-war movements, it has left many people wondering about how the man who led the largest military force in our history could give such a speech at all.

As Eisenhower's public record shows, he was not an isolationist, and throughout his presidency he had favored robust military spending. But in this speech he was calling for *balance*.

Robert Gates, a Kansan who served as secretary of defense between December 2006 and July 2011, kept a picture of Eisenhower in his office. In a 2010 speech at the Eisenhower Library to celebrate the sixty-fifth anniversary of the Allied victory in Europe, Gates said: "Does the number of warships we have, and are building, really put America at risk when the U.S. battle fleet is larger than the next thirteen navies combined—eleven of which are our partners and allies? Is it a dire threat that by 2020, the United States will have only twenty-times more advanced stealth fighters than China?" When is enough, enough?

Eisenhower spoke about these same issues during his entire presidency. He looked at the national budget as a whole and tried to focus on the needs of the country. He believed that the national interest—including national security—could not be measured by the number of weapons we had, but by the stability of the nation. Having a healthy economy was a national security issue. So were civil rights, education, and infrastructure. Our greatness as a nation, not just our military might, was our best protection against the dangers of the world.

Ike knew that bigger isn't always better or smarter—and this might be truer than ever now. Today, our defense needs are more diverse, and the number of weapons we have does not necessarily give us an edge in fighting terrorism.

During World War II, the Allies did not win the

D-Day campaign simply because of overwhelming force, although we had that. It was also a matter of brilliant strategy. Ike prized his advisors and welcomed even the most heated debates, believing that some of the best ideas came out of dissent.

In 2011, David Eisenhower, Ike's grandson, wrote an article titled "A Tale of Two Speeches" for the *Los Angeles Times*. In it, he reflected on the two men—presidents Eisenhower and Kennedy—who gave historic speeches within three days of one another in 1961. The author observed that the two men were political opponents from different parties and with great contrasts in style and philosophy. Despite these key differences, both "addresses converged on key points, namely on questions of citizenship in the modern age and on the belief that the American system of self government can rise to any challenge." It's a message his grandfather would have approved of.

APPENDIX: EISENHOWER'S FAREWELL ADDRESS TO THE NATION

JANUARY 17, 1961

GOOD EVENING, MY FELLOW Americans.

First, I should like to express my gratitude to the radio and television networks for the opportunities they have given me over the years to bring reports and messages to our nation. My special thanks go to them for the opportunity of addressing you this evening.

Three days from now, after half a century in the service of our country, I shall lay down the responsibilities of office as, in traditional and solemn ceremony, the authority of the presidency is vested in my successor. This evening, I come to you with a message of leave-taking and farewell, and to share a few final thoughts with you, my countrymen.

Like every other citizen, I wish the new president, and all who will labor with him, Godspeed. I pray that the coming years will be blessed with peace and prosperity for all.

Our people expect their president and the Congress to find essential agreement on issues of great moment, the wise resolution of which will better shape the future of the nation. My own relations with the Congress, which began on a remote and tenuous basis when, long ago, a member of the Senate appointed me to West Point, have since ranged to the intimate during the war and immediate postwar period, and finally to the mutually interdependent during these past eight years. In this final relationship, the Congress and the administration have, on most vital issues, cooperated well, to serve the national good, rather than mere partisanship, and so have assured that the business of the nation should go forward. So, my official relationship with the Congress ends in a feeling—on my part—of gratitude that we have been able to do so much together.

We now stand ten years past the midpoint of a century that has witnessed four major wars among great nations. Three of these involved our own country. Despite these holocausts, America is today the strongest, the most influential, and most productive nation in the world. Understandably proud of this preeminence, we yet realize that America's leadership and prestige depend, not merely upon our unmatched material progress, riches, and military strength, but on how we use our power in the interests of world peace and human betterment.

Throughout America's adventure in free government, our basic purposes have been to keep the peace, to foster progress in human achievement, and to enhance liberty, dignity, and integrity among people and among nations. To strive for less would be unworthy of a free and religious people. Any failure traceable to arrogance, or our lack of comprehension, or readiness to sacrifice would inflict upon us grievous hurt, both at home and abroad.

Progress toward these noble goals is persistently threatened by the conflict now engulfing the world. It commands our whole attention, absorbs our very beings. We face a hostile ideology global in scope, atheistic in character, ruthless in purpose, and insidious in method. Unhappily, the danger it poses promises to be of indefinite duration. To meet it successfully, there is called for, not so much the emotional and transitory sacrifices of crisis, but rather those which enable us to carry forward steadily, surely, and without complaint the burdens of a prolonged and complex struggle with liberty the stake. Only thus shall we remain, despite every provocation, on our charted course toward permanent peace and human betterment.

Crises there will continue to be. In meeting them, whether foreign or domestic, great or small, there is a recurring temptation to feel that some spectacular and costly action could become the miraculous solution to all current difficulties. A huge increase in newer elements of our defenses; development of unrealistic programs to cure every ill in agriculture; a dramatic expansion in basic and applied research—these and many other possibilities, each possibly promising in itself, may be suggested as the only way to the road we wish to travel.

But each proposal must be weighed in the light of a broader consideration: the need to maintain balance in and among national programs, balance between the private in and among national programs, balance between the private and the public economy, balance between the cost and hoped-for advantages, balance between the clearly necessary and the comfortably desirable, balance between our essential requirements as a nation and the duties imposed by the nation upon the individuals, balance between actions of the moment and the national welfare of the future. Good judgment seeks balance and progress. Lack of it eventually finds imbalance and frustration. The record of many decades stands as proof that our people and their government have, in the main, understood these truths and have responded to them well, in the face of threat and stress.

But threats, new in kind or degree, constantly arise. Of these, I mention two only.

A vital element in keeping the peace is our military establishment. Our arms must be mighty, ready for instant action, so that no potential aggressor may be tempted to risk his own destruction. Our military organization today bears little relation to that known of any of my predecessors in peacetime, or, indeed, by the fighting men of World War II or Korea.

Until the latest of our world conflicts, the United States had no armaments industry. American makers of plowshares could, with time and as required, make swords as well. But we can no longer risk emergency improvisation of national defense. We have been compelled to create a permanent armaments industry of vast proportions. Added to this, three and a half million men and women are directly engaged in the defense establishment. We annually spend on military security alone more than the net income of all United States corporations.

Now this conjunction of an immense military establishment and a large arms industry is new in the American experience. The total influence—economic, political, even spiritual—is felt in every city, every statehouse, every office of the federal government. We recognize the imperative need for this development. Yet, we must not fail to comprehend its grave implications. Our toil, resources, and livelihood are all involved. So is the very structure of our society.

In the councils of government, we must guard against

the acquisition of unwarranted influence, whether sought or unsought, by the military-industrial complex. The potential for the disastrous rise of misplaced power exists and will persist. We must never let the weight of this combination endanger our liberties or democratic processes. We should take nothing for granted. Only an alert and knowledgeable citizenry can compel the proper meshing of the huge industrial and military machinery of defense with our peaceful methods and goals, so that security and liberty may prosper together.

Akin to, and largely responsible for the sweeping changes in our industrial-military posture, has been the technological revolution during recent decades. In this revolution, research has become central; it also becomes more formalized, complex, and costly. A steadily increasing share is conducted for, by, or at the direction of, the federal government.

Today, the solitary inventor, tinkering in his shop, has been overshadowed by task forces of scientists in laboratories and testing fields. In the same fashion, the free university, historically the fountainhead of free ideas and scientific discovery, has experienced a revolution in the conduct of research. Partly because of the huge costs involved, a government contract becomes virtually a substitute for intellectual curiosity. For every old blackboard there are now hundreds of new electronic computers. The prospect of domination of the nation's scholars by federal employment, project allocations, and the power of money is ever present—and is gravely to be regarded.

Yet, in holding scientific research and discovery in respect, as we should, we must also be alert to the equal and opposite danger that public policy could itself become the captive of a scientific-technological elite.

It is the task of statesmanship to mold, to balance, and to integrate these and other forces, new and old, within the principles of our democratic system—ever aiming toward the supreme goals of our free society.

Another factor in maintaining balance involves the element of time. As we peer into society's future, we—you and I, and our government—must avoid the impulse to live only for today, plundering for our own ease and convenience the precious resources of tomorrow. We cannot mortgage the material assets of our grandchildren without risking the loss also of their political and spiritual heritage. We want democracy to survive for all generations to come, not to become the insolvent phantom of tomorrow.

Down the long lane of the history yet to be written, America knows that this world of ours, ever growing smaller, must avoid becoming a community of dreadful fear and hate, and be, instead, a proud confederation of mutual trust and respect. Such a confederation must be one of equals. The weakest must come to the conference table with the same confidence as do we, protected as we are by our moral, economic, and military strength. That table, though scarred by many past frustrations, cannot be abandoned for the certain agony of the battlefield.

Disarmament, with mutual honor and confidence, is a continuing imperative. Together we must learn how to compose difference, not with arms, but with intellect and decent purpose. Because this need is so sharp and apparent, I confess that I lay down my official responsibilities in this field with a definite sense of disappointment. As one who has witnessed the horror and the lingering sadness of war, as one who knows that another war could utterly destroy this civilization which has been so slowly and painfully built over thousands of years, I wish I could say tonight that a lasting peace is in sight.

Happily, I can say that war has been avoided. Steady progress toward our ultimate goals has been made. But so much remains to be done. As a private citizen, I shall never cease to do what little I can to help the world advance along that road.

So, in this, my last good night to you as your president, I thank you for the many opportunities you have given me for public service in war and in peace. I trust that in that service you find some things worthy. As for the rest of it, I know you will find ways to improve performance in the future.

You and I, my fellow citizens, need to be strong in our faith that all nations, under God, will reach the goal of peace with justice. May we be ever unswerving in devotion to principle, confident but humble with power, diligent in pursuit of the nation's great goals.

To all the peoples of the world, I once more give expression to America's prayerful and continuing aspiration: We pray that peoples of all faiths, all races, all nations, may have their great human needs satisfied; that those now denied opportunity shall come to enjoy it to the full; that all who yearn for freedom may experience its spiritual blessings. Those who have freedom will understand, also, its heavy responsibility; that all who are insensitive to the needs of others will learn charity; that the scourges of poverty, disease, and ignorance will be made to disappear from the earth; and that in the goodness of time, all people will come to live together in a peace guaranteed by the binding force of mutual respect and love.

Now, on Friday noon, I am to become a private citizen. I am proud to do so. I look forward to it.

Thank you, and good night.

— ACKNOWLEDGMENTS —

PRESIDENT EISENHOWER KNEW HOW to tap into the power of others, to encourage them to be their best, to work toward an objective, and to make sure they got credit. This book could not have happened without the amazing work and writing of my co-author, Catherine Whitney. Her tireless hours of work and research, and her ability to capture my voice and writing style as we bounced copy back and forth, refining every last word, has been remarkable. From the first time we sat down to walk through the premise and scope of the book, Catherine had a gleam in her eye that rediscovering Eisenhower was as important to her as it was to me. She lived, breathed, and slept Eisenhower for many months, and this book is the result of that dedication. Catherine is a real pro.

A special thank-you to Sydney Soderberg, our researcher at the library in Abilene, who was invaluable as well. Sydney helped us find nuggets of information inside the vast expanse of documents and oral histories that really made the book come to life. In a true Kansas way, Sydney welcomed us like we were family every visit we made to Abilene. A former mayor of nearby Salina, Sydney could be doing anything she wanted—but we were ecstatic she signed on to dig out research treasures about Ike for us.

I am particularly grateful for the tremendous support of the staff at the Eisenhower Library and Museum in Abilene. Thank you to former director Karl M. Weissenbach and Tim Rives, the current acting director, who both helped me formulate the idea for the book. Thanks to William Snyder, curator of the museum; Samantha Kerner, communications director; and Kathy Struss, audiovisual archivist. The John F. Kennedy Library and the Truman Library were also instrumental in our research. In particular, I want to thank Maryrose Grossman, audio/visual archivist at the John F. Kennedy Library.

The Columbia University Oral History Project's dedication to preserving the voices of previous administrations is a noble effort—and it made Ike's presidency feel as if it were happening in real time. Very special thanks to David A. Olson, archivist for the Columbia Center for Oral History, Rare Book and Manuscript Library, Columbia University.

Writers of history stand on the shoulders of many others, and I am deeply grateful for the rich library of books and media about Ike's life, produced by authors, editors, documentarians, photographers, and others, who endeavored, as I have, to shine a bright light on Ike's important legacy. These contributions, including those of Ike's grandchildren, have meant a great deal to me.

As always, deep appreciation to my manager, Larry Kramer, and book agent, Claudia Cross with Folio Literary Management, for their encouragement and excellent handling of day-to-day logistics. I'm blessed to have such a strong team.

Special thanks to Peter Hubbard, my editor at William Morrow for the adult version. From the start, he grasped my vision for the book, and his dedication, patience, and insight have been invaluable. My deepest appreciation to Peter and to the entire team at William Morrow.

For the Young Readers' Edition, many thanks to the writer Winifred Conkling, who adapted the text, and to editors Alexandra Cooper and Alyssa Miele for making this a book young people can enjoy and learn from.

I am also grateful to my employer, Fox News, for allowing me the leeway to spend time on this valuable project, and for being supportive of my efforts.

And a very special thanks to my family—my wife,

Amy, and my sons, Paul and Daniel—for their constant support and sacrifices while I was working on this project. I am gratified that Paul and Daniel will be able to read this book, written especially for them and their peers.

Hopefully, this book will bring the thirty-fourth president of the United States into new focus for a new generation. We can ALWAYS learn from our past.

— GLOSSARY —

ALLIED POWERS: The nations that formed an alliance to resist aggression from the Axis powers during World War II; the three largest countries—the United States, the United Kingdom, and the Soviet Union—controlled Allied strategy; other member countries included China, France, Poland, India, Austria, and Canada, among others.

AXIS POWERS: Germany, Italy, Japan, and the other countries that fought against the Allies during World War II

BAY OF PIGS INVASION: A failed mission by a Central Intelligence Agency (CIA)–backed group to overthrow Cuban leader Fidel Castro's communist regime in April 1961

COLD WAR: The period from 1947 to 1991 when the relationship between the United States and the Soviet Union was characterized by tension and distrust

CUBAN MISSILE CRISIS: A thirteen-day showdown—October 16–28, 1962—between the United States and the Soviet Union over the presence of Soviet nuclear missiles in Cuba and American missiles in Turkey and Italy

McCARTHYISM: A campaign against alleged communists led by Senator Joseph McCarthy in the period from 1950 to 1954

MILITARY-INDUSTRIAL COMPLEX: The mutually beneficial relationship between the military and the industries that produce arms and defense systems

MISSILE GAP: The perception that that Soviet Union was developing and stockpiling intercontinental-range ballistic missiles in greater numbers than that of the United States

NATO (NORTH AMERICAN TREATY ORGANIZATION): The alliance of twenty-nine countries from North America and Europe that was established in 1949; a key provision of the treaty is that an attack against one of its members will be considered an attack against all.

NEW FRONTIER: The term used by John F. Kennedy to characterize his administration; it was first used when Kennedy accepted the presidential nomination at the Democratic National Convention in 1960.

OPERATION OVERLORD: The military code name for the Allied operation that launched the invasion of German-occupied Western Europe during World War II

POLITBURO: The policy-making committee of the Communist Party in the former Soviet Union

VICHY FRANCE: The French state headed by Philippe Pétain during World War II, from the Nazi German invasion of France to the Allied liberation at the end of the war

— SOURCE NOTES —

CHAPTER 1: THE FIRST VISIT

8 *"The general doesn't know any more . . ."*: Reported in *Kansas City Times*, October 24, 1952.

8 *"I wonder if I can stand . . ."*: Emmet John Hughes, *The Ordeal of Power: A Political Memoir of the Eisenhower Years* (London: Macmillan, 1975).

9 *"Ike's boy"*: Dwight D. Eisenhower, *Waging Peace: The White House Years, 1956–1961* (Garden City, NY: Doubleday, 1965).

11 *"We are facing a gap on which . . ."*: Speech by John F. Kennedy on national defense in the U.S. Senate, February 1960, as he was launching his presidential campaign, John F. Kennedy Library and Museum.

11 *"Mr. President, it's good to be here"*: James Hagerty notes from the meeting, Dwight D. Eisenhower Library.

CHAPTER 2: BECOMING IKE

15 *"If I'm lucky, I'll be a colonel"*: Oral history interview with Mamie Eisenhower by Maclyn Burg and John Wickman, July 15–16, 1972, p. 70, Dwight D. Eisenhower Library.

18 *"I was raised in a little town . . ."*: Eisenhower's remarks upon receiving the Democratic Legacy Award at B'nai B'rith dinner in honor of the fortieth anniversary of the Anti-Defamation League, November 25, 1953.

19 *"He that conquereth his own soul . . ."*: Dwight D. Eisenhower, *At Ease: Stories I Tell to Friends* (Garden City, NY: Doubleday, 1967).

20 *"anger drawer"*: Ibid.

21 *"I'd rather be dead than crippled . . ."*: Ibid.

21 *"Dear Sir, I would very much like . . ."*: Letter to Senator Bristow, August 20, 1910, and October 25, 1910, on file in the Dwight D. Eisenhower Library.

22 *"Dad was at work when Ike left . . ."*: Interview with Milton Eisenhower at childhood home by Maclyn Burg, October 15, 1971, Dwight D. Eisenhower Library.

22 *"Practice hitting my way for a year . . ."*: Eisenhower, *At Ease*.

23 *"the class the stars fell upon"*: Michael E. Haskew, *West Point 1915: Eisenhower, Bradley, and the Class the Stars Fell On* (Minneapolis: Zenith, 2014).

25 *"a tragedy from which we never recovered"*: Merle Miller, *Ike the Soldier: As They Knew Him* (New York: Putnam, 1987).

26 *"This is the best officer in the army . . ."*: Efficiency Report Dwight D. Eisenhower—0-3822—Major Infantry,

records at the Dwight D. Eisenhower Library.

27 *"You do not lead by hitting . . .":* Emmet John Hughes, *The Ordeal of Power: A Political Memoir of the Eisenhower Years* (New York: Atheneum, 1963).

29 *"I certainly do want to read it . . .":* Eisenhower, *At Ease.*

CHAPTER 3: IKE IN COMMAND

31 *"We are in this together as Allies . . .":* Dwight D. Eisenhower, *Crusade in Europe* (Garden City, NY: Doubleday, 1948).

32 *"Well, Ike, you are going to command Overlord":* Ibid.

32 *"Mr. President, I realize that such an appointment . . .":* Ibid.

33 *"He's not the greatest soldier in the world . . .":* Joseph E. Persico, *Roosevelt's Centurions: FDR and the Commanders He Led to Victory in World War II* (New York: Random House, 2013).

35 *"Soldiers like to see the men who are directing operations":* Eisenhower, *At Ease.*

36 *"Okay, we'll go":* There are a number of versions about what Ike actually said in that moment. In his analysis of the record, "Like Footprints in the Sand: Searching for Eisenhower's Climactic D-Day Words," Tim Rives, the deputy director of the Dwight D. Eisenhower Presidential Library, cites a few of the versions.

36 *"Soldiers, Sailors and Airmen . . .":* Eisenhower's order of

the day, June 6, 1944, Dwight D. Eisenhower Library.

37 *"I have withdrawn the troops . . .":* Eisenhower's written apology in the event of Overlord's failure is at the Dwight D. Eisenhower Library and on display at the museum.

38 *"How in the world did you have the nerve . . .":* Oral history interview with Mamie Eisenhower by Maclyn Burg and John Wickman, July 15–16, 1972, p. 112, Dwight D. Eisenhower Library.

38 *"The present situation is to be regarded . . .":* Eisenhower, *Crusade in Europe.*

39 *"General, there is nothing that you may want . . .":* Jean Edward Smith, *Eisenhower in War and Peace* (New York: Random House, 2012); also oral history with John S. D. Eisenhower by Carol Hegeman, January 26, 1984, Eisenhower National Historic Site, National Park Service.

40 *"I voiced to him my grave misgivings . . .":* Dwight D. Eisenhower, *Mandate for Change: The White House Years 1953–1956* (Garden City, NY: Doubleday, 1965).

CHAPTER 4: A NONPOLITICIAN RUNS FOR PRESIDENT

41 *"I felt that the Republican Party . . .":* Oral history with Thomas E. Dewey by Pauline Madow, December 1, 1970, p. 2, Columbia University Oral History

Project, Dwight D. Eisenhower Library.

44 *"He was absolutely devoted to doing anything . . .":* Oral history with Milton Eisenhower by Robert F. Ivanov, November 6, 1975, p. 34, Columbia University Oral History Project, Dwight D. Eisenhower Library.

45 *"You know, Governor, there isn't anything . . .":* Oral history interview with Sherman Adams by Michael Birkner, March 3, 1985, Columbia University Oral History Project, Dwight D. Eisenhower Library.

45 *"They knew that he was honest . . .":* Oral history, Milton Eisenhower.

48 *"Politics is a funny thing . . .":* Oral history with James Hagerty by Ed Edwin, March 2, 1967, Columbia University Oral History Project, Dwight D. Eisenhower Library.

49 *"What do you mean I'm not going into the South . . .":* Oral history with James Hagerty by Ed Edwin, March 2, 1967, Columbia University Oral History Project, Dwight D. Eisenhower Library; also oral history interview with Sherman Adams by Ed Edwin, April 10, 1967, pp. 85–86; Columbia University Oral History Project, Dwight D. Eisenhower Library.

49 *"eager to play the role of a front man to traitors":* Oral history with James Hagerty.

49 *"a conspiracy on a scale so immense . . .":* Harry S. Truman Library and Museum.

50 *"I had never thought the man who is now . . ."*: Remarks by Harry Truman in Batavia, NY, October 10, 1952, Harry S. Truman Library and Museum.

50 *"I will clean up the mess in Washington . . ."*: Milton Eisenhower, *The President Is Calling: A Veteran Advisor for the Presidency Suggests Far-Reaching Changes* (Garden City, NY: Doubleday, 1974).

51 *"throw him off the ticket"*: Oral history with John Eisenhower by Carol Hegeman, January 26, 1984, p. 39, Columbia University Oral History Project, Eisenhower National Historical Site, National Park Service.

51 *"too political"*: Ibid.

52 *"I shall go to Korea"*: Oral history with James Hagerty by Ed Edwin, March 2, 1967, pp. 56–57, Columbia University Oral History Project, Dwight D. Eisenhower Library.

54 *"Oh, Mrs. Eisenhower . . ."*: Oral history interview with Mamie Eisenhower by Maclyn Burg and John Wickman, July 15–16, 1972, p. 152, Dwight D. Eisenhower Library.

55 *"clear and definite solution to the Korean conflict"*: Eisenhower, *Mandate for Change.*

55 *"I appreciate your announced readiness to discuss . . ."*: Ibid.

55 *"This is the first time that the slightest official interest . . ."*:

The exchange provoked a flurry of newspaper articles, such as this overly optimistic front page of the New York *Monthly Bulletin*, December 11, 1952: "Exchange of Messages Solves Far East Problems."

CHAPTER 5: GENTLE BUT STRONG

57 *"I did":* Carl M. Brauer, *Presidential Transitions: Eisenhower Through Reagan* (New York: Oxford University Press, 1986); also *Harry S. Truman, Off the Record: The Private Papers of Harry S. Truman* (Columbia: University of Missouri Press, 1997).

58 *"If I'd told you to come, you would have been there":* Brauer, *Presidential Transitions.*

58 *"Almighty God, as we stand here . . .":* The Inaugural Addresses of Twentieth-Century American Presidents (New York: Praeger, 1993).

62 *"hidden hand":* Fred I. Greenstein, *The Hidden-Hand Presidency: Eisenhower as a Leader* (1982; reprint, Baltimore: Johns Hopkins University Press, 1994).

63 *"You can't defeat Communism by destroying America":* Oral history with James Hagerty.

66 *"If you run I will vote for you":* Oral history with Lucius D. Clay by Jean Smith, April 17, 1971, p. 929, Columbia University Oral History Project, Dwight D. Eisenhower Library.

68 *"I want to speak to you about the serious situation . . .":*

Eisenhower speech, sending troops to Little Rock, Dwight D. Eisenhower Library.

CHAPTER 6: GOOD EVENING, MY FELLOW AMERICANS

75 *"You know that General MacArthur got quite . . .":* As an example, Moos cited MacArthur's famous Guild Hall speech in London. Oral history with Malcolm Moos by T. H. Baker, November 2, 1972, Columbia University Oral History Project, Dwight D. Eisenhower Library.

76 *"I think you've got something here":* Oral history with Malcolm Moos by T. H. Baker, November 2, 1972, p. 18, Columbia University Oral History Project, Dwight D. Eisenhower Library.

77 *"military-industrial-scientific complex":* The various drafts of Eisenhower's farewell address are available at the Eisenhower Library and online at www.eisen hower.archives.gov.

78 *"military-industrial-congressional complex":* Ibid.

79 *"You've done so much for me . . .":* Oral history with Wilton Persons by Stephen J. Wayne, May 29, 1974, Columbia University Oral History Project, Dwight D. Eisenhower Library.

CHAPTER 7: WORKING TOGETHER

83 *"In this final relationship . . .":* Farewell address drafts,

speech file, Dwight D. Eisenhower Library.

84 *"Good man, but wrong business":* Recounted in Harry S. Truman, *Memoirs, Vol. 2, 1946–1962: Years of Trial and Hope* (New York: Da Capo, 1955).

87 *"Mr. President, when I agree with you . . .":* Johnson quoted himself saying this to Eisenhower in his White House tapes. Michael Beschloss, *Reaching for Glory: Lyndon Johnson's Secret White House Tapes 1964–1965* (New York: Simon & Schuster, 2001).

89 *"The problems a president faces . . .":* "Republicans: The Loneliness of Office," *Time,* November 14, 1960.

CHAPTER 8: DEALING WITH THE SOVIET UNION

90 *"a permanent peace with justice":* White House press conference, January 18, 1961.

90 *"flame brightly until at last . . .":* Eisenhower's Second Inaugural Address, January 20, 1957, Eisenhower Library.

91 *"If they're easy, they're solved down . . .":* Oral history with James Hagerty by Ed Edwin, March 2, 1967, Columbia University Oral History Project, Dwight D. Eisenhower Library.

91 *"The uneven development of capitalist countries usually leads . . .":* From the Pamphlet Collection, J. Stalin, *Speeches Delivered at Meetings of Voters of the Stalin Electoral District, Moscow* (Moscow: Foreign Languages Publishing House, 1950).

92 *"barbarians":* Speech to the American Legion at Madison Square Garden, New York, August 25, 1952.

92 *"hope for peace among men . . .":* Ibid.

93 *"I would meet anybody, anywhere . . .":* Oral history with James Hagerty.

93 *"The thoughts of America go out . . .":* Message from the president on the death of Stalin, Dwight D. Eisenhower Library.

94 *"Every gun that is made, every warship launched . . .":* "The Chance for Peace," Dwight D. Eisenhower Library.

95 *"It must be the policy of the United States to support . . .":* Truman's letter to Secretary of State James Byrnes, January 5, 1946.

96 *"not worth fighting":* Dwight D. Eisenhower Library.

97 *"make a serious bid for peace":* Ibid.

97 *"With malice toward none . . .":* Dwight D. Eisenhower Library.

97 *"This is our resolve and our dedication":* Eisenhower Address on Korean Armistice, August 23, 1953, Eisenhower Library.

98 *"You have a row of dominoes set up . . .":* Oral history with Charles Halleck by Thomas Soapes, April 26, 1977, Columbia University Oral History Project, Dwight D. Eisenhower Library; also oral history with James Hagerty by Ed Edwin, March 2, 1967,

Columbia University Oral History Project, Dwight D. Eisenhower Library.

98 *"I am not going to land any American troops . . .":* Eisenhower, *Mandate.*

98 *"Vietnam represents the cornerstone . . .":* Speech to the Conference on Vietnam luncheon, at the Hotel Willard in Washington, DC, June 1, 1956.

100 *"No, no, no . . .":* Vladislav M. Zubok, "Soviet Policy Aims at the Geneva Conference, 1955," in Gunter Bischof and Saki Dockrill, eds., *Cold War Respite: The Geneva Summit of 1955* (Baton Rouge: Louisiana State University Press, 2000).

101–2 *"We have apartments in Russia . . .":* Oral history with Admiral Evan P. Aurand by John T. Mason Jr., May 1, 1967, pp. 111–112, Columbia University Oral History Project, Dwight D. Eisenhower Library.

102 *"All I can assure you is that you will get fair treatment . . .":* Oral history with James Hagerty by Ed Edwin, March 2, 1967, Columbia University Oral History Project, Dwight D. Eisenhower Library.

102 *"Yes, but what are you going to tell them to say?":* Ibid.

102 *"When Stalin was still alive . . .":* W. Dale Nelson, *The President Is at Camp David* (Syracuse, NY: Syracuse University Press, 1995).

103 *"The possibility of war with the Russians . . .":* David Eisenhower with Julie Nixon Eisenhower, *Going*

Home to Glory: A Memoir of Life with Dwight D. Eisenhower 1961–1969 (New York: Simon & Schuster, 2010).

103 *"At that conference with the president's grandchildren . . .":* "Khrushchev Speaks of His Gettysburg Visit," National Press Club, September 27, 1959, Dwight D. Eisenhower Library.

CHAPTER 9: CONFRONTING THE NUCLEAR THREAT

107 *"I don't want to be the president of a nation . . .":* Oral history with Milton Eisenhower by John Luter, September 6, 1967, pp. 41–43, Columbia University Oral History Project, Dwight D. Eisenhower Library.

109 *"The very least we can say is that, looking ten years ahead . . .":* J. Robert Oppenheimer, "Atomic Weapons and American Policy," *Foreign Affairs* 21, no. 4 (July 1953).

110 *"Of course, this is something we can never resort to . . .":* Oral history with James Hagerty by Ed Edwin, March 2, 1967, Columbia University Oral History Project, Dwight D. Eisenhower Library.

111 *"If the Russians press us on Berlin . . .":* Oral history with Howard K. Smith by John Luter, January 19, 1967, p. 14, Columbia University Oral History Project, Dwight D. Eisenhower Library.

111 *"To stop there would be to accept helplessly . . .":*

Presidential speech file, Dwight D. Eisenhower Library.

114 *"a fallout shelter for everyone"*: Kennedy speech, October 1961; also oral history with Admiral Evan P. Aurand by John T. Mason Jr., May 1, 1967, Columbia University Oral History Project, Dwight D. Eisenhower Library; also Kenneth D. Rose, *One Nation Underground: The Fallout Shelter in American Culture* (New York: New York University Press, 2001).

116 *"We must not return to the 'crash-program' psychology . . ."*: Eisenhower's State of the Union, 1961, Dwight D. Eisenhower Library.

117 *"Well, I don't know if you could put it that way . . ."*: Eisenhower's final press conference, Dwight D. Eisenhower Library.

CHAPTER 10: THE MILITARY-INDUSTRIAL COMPLEX

124 *"Mr. Nixon has suggested that if he is elected president . . ."*: Kennedy campaign speech, John F. Kennedy Presidential Library.

125 *"Surely, it is impressive that the old soldier should make this warning . . ."*: Walter Lippman, "Today and Tomorrow: Eisenhower's Farewell Warning," *Washington Post*, January 19, 1961.

CHAPTER 11: GETTING TO KNOW PRESIDENT-ELECT KENNEDY

137 *"Ike, for the good of the country, you cannot let . . .":* Oral history with Malcolm Moos by T. H. Baker, November 2, 1972, pp. 29–30. Columbia University Oral History Project, Dwight D. Eisenhower Library.

140 *"One of my biggest concerns is that government . . .":* Oral history with Clark Clifford by Larry J. Hackman, December 16, 1974, John F. Kennedy Library.

142 *"numerous instances of malfeasance in office . . .":* Richard E. Neustadt, *Presidential Power: The Politics of Leadership* (Cambridge: Cambridge University Press, 1960).

143 *"Very interesting. Now we'll wait . . .":* Tom Wicker, "State of the Union; Dirksen . . . Democrats Critical of Message, G.O.P. Applauds Statesmanship," *New York Times*, January 12, 1961.

144 *"I came this morning not to say goodbye . . .":* Final news conference, transcript, American Presidency Project, http://www.presidency.ucsb.edu.

145 *"Well, now, you know, that's the last thing . . .":* Ibid.

145 *"I'd say in a peaceful world and enjoying . . .":* Final press conference transcript, Dwight D. Eisenhower Library.

CHAPTER 12: THE DAY BEFORE

146 *"If I've done nothing else for this country . . .":* Christopher

Matthews, *Kennedy and Nixon: The Rivalry That Shaped Postwar America* (New York: Simon & Schuster, 1996).

147 *"If you give me a week, I might think . . .":* Ike told Merriman Smith he didn't mean it that way. Basically, he overthought the question. Oral history with Merriman Smith by John Luter, January 3, 1968, pp. 44–45, Columbia University Oral History Project, Dwight D. Eisenhower Library; also, Gabriel Hauge pointed out that Ike "would never undercut anyone in public," so it's unlikely he meant it as a slam against Nixon. Oral history with Gabriel Hauge by Ed Edwin, March 10, 1967, p. 117, Columbia University Oral History Project, Dwight D. Eisenhower Library.

147 *"The President is a man of integrity . . .":* Ann Whitman Diary Series, August 30, 1960, Dwight D. Eisenhower Library.

147 *"The passage of years has taken me out . . .":* Personal letter to Richard Nixon, Dwight D. Eisenhower Library.

148 *"This is the first time in one hundred years . . .":* Nixon's remarks to the Senate, Dwight D. Eisenhower Library.

149 *"Opal Drill Three":* Dwight D. Eisenhower, *Waging Peace: The White House Years 1956–1961* (Garden City, NY: Doubleday, 1965).

149 *"Neither of us apparently felt any impulse . . .":* Accounts from both Eisenhower and Kennedy; Eisenhower, *Waging Peace*; Kennedy, a dictated account, John F. Kennedy Presidential Library.

150 *"We cannot let Laos fall to the Communists even . . .":* Ibid.

151 *"Before you came to power you indicated . . .":* Michael H. Hunt, *Ideology and U.S. Foreign Policy* (New Haven, CT: Yale University Press, 1987).

152 *"They saw him as a champion of the downtrodden . . .":* Eisenhower, *Waging Peace*.

153 *"If you can't stand up to Castro . . .":* Kennedy campaign speech in Johnstown, Pennsylvania, October 15, 1960, John F. Kennedy Library.

154 *"Thank you for giving us everything we asked for . . .":* Accounts from both Eisenhower and Kennedy; Eisenhower, *Waging Peace*; Kennedy, a dictated account, John F. Kennedy Presidential Library.

155 *"That Old Black Magic":* Todd Purdum, "From That Day Forth," *Vanity Fair*, January 17, 2011.

CHAPTER 13: THE PASSAGE

160 *"You must have a hot speech":* Thurston Clarke, *Ask Not: The Inauguration of John F. Kennedy and the Speech That Changed America* (New York: Henry Holt, 2004).

161 *"Ask not what you can do . . .":* Ibid.; also, Richard Tofel, *Sounding the Trumpet: The Making of John F. Kennedy's Inaugural Address* (Chicago: Ivan R. Dee, 2005).

161 *"Having no satisfactory answer . . .":* Ibid.

162 *"The president of the United States, naturally, must be ready . . .":* Ike's speech at the Lotos Club, New York City, December 6, 1962.

162 *"The Eisenhower concern, as I read it . . .":* Edward Bliss Jr., ed, *In Search of Light: The Broadcasts of Edward R. Murrow* (London: Palgrave Macmillan, 1968).

162 *"was, in fact, suggesting that the machine . . .":* Ibid.

163 *"we shall pay any price, bear any burden . . .":* John F. Kennedy inaugural address, John F. Kennedy Presidential Library.

164 *"Leaving the White House will not be easy . . .":* David Eisenhower with Julie Nixon Eisenhower, *Going Home to Glory: A Memoir of Life with Dwight D. Eisenhower 1961–1969* (New York: Simon & Schuster, 2010).

165 *"My dear Mr. President, On my first day in office . . .":* Letter from Kennedy, Dwight D. Eisenhower Library.

166 *"There's something wrong with the telephone . . .":* Oral history with Merriman Smith by John Luter, January 2, 1968, pp. 69–71, Columbia University Oral

History Project, Dwight D. Eisenhower Library.

167 *"I don't see what's wrong with it . . .":* Ibid.

168 *"hour of peril":* President Kennedy's first State of the Union address, John F. Kennedy Presidential Library.

168 *"Organization cannot make a genius out of an incompetent . . .":* Dwight D. Eisenhower, *Mandate for Change: The White House Years 1953–1956* (Garden City, NY: Doubleday, 1965).

CHAPTER 14: A SPRING DAY AT CAMP DAVID

170 *"When I saw them together that day . . .":* W. Dale Nelson, *The President Is at Camp David* (Syracuse, NY: Syracuse University Press, 1995).

171 *"For God's sake be careful . . .":* Oral history with Samuel E. Belk by William M. Moss, June 1, 1974, John F. Kennedy Library.

173 *"No one knows how tough this job is . . .":* Dwight D. Eisenhower, *Waging Peace: The White House Years 1956–1961* (Garden City, NY: Doubleday, 1965).

173 *"he seemed himself at that moment":* Ibid.

173 *"Well, I just approved a plan . . .":* Ibid.

173 *"Mr. President, before you approved this plan . . .":* Ibid.

174 *"Mr. President, were there any changes in the plan . . .":* Ibid.

174 *"We felt it necessary that we keep our hand . . .":* Thomas Preston, *The President and His Inner Circle: Leadership Style and the Advisory Process in Foreign Affairs* (New

York: Columbia University Press, 2001).

174 *"Mr. President, how could you expect the world to believe . . .":* Ibid.

175 *"I asked President Eisenhower here to bring him up to date . . .":* Eisenhower, *Diaries*; Eisenhower, *Waging Peace*; interview transcript of Eisenhower discussing his meeting with Kennedy, conducted by Captain A. Ross Wollen for the *Pointer*, a publication of the Corps of Cadets, West Point, New York, Dwight D. Eisenhower Post-Presidential Papers, 1965, Dwight D. Eisenhower Library.

175 *"I am all in favor of the United States supporting the man . . .":* Ibid.

177 *"It is up to the U.S. to decide whether there will be war . . .":* Frederick Kempe, *Kennedy, Khrushchev, and the Most Dangerous Place on Earth—Berlin 1961* (New York: Simon & Schuster, 1993).

178 *"In our discussion and exchanges on Berlin . . .":* Kennedy's letter to Khrushchev, Cuban Missile Crisis, John F. Kennedy Presidential Library.

179 *"I hope that the United States Government will display wisdom . . .":* Khrushchev's letter, Cuban Missile Crisis, John F. Kennedy Presidential Library.

179 *"What about if the Soviet Union—Khrushchev . . .":* Recording of telephone conversation, dictation belt 30.2, John F. Kennedy Library.

180 *"You, Mr. President, are not declaring a quarantine . . ."*: John F. Kennedy Presidential Library.

181 *"Now the only thing I would suggest, Mr. President . . ."*: Recording, microsites, jfklibrary.org.cmc/oct28/doc3 .html.

183 *"I need you more than ever now"*: November 23, 1960, Presidential Papers of Lyndon B. Johnson, LBJ Library.

184 *"Point out first that you have come to this office . . ."*: Ibid.

186 *"No one could hate war more than I . . ."*: David Eisenhower with Julie Nixon Eisenhower, *Going Home to Glory: A Memoir of Life with Dwight D. Eisenhower 1961–1969* (New York: Simon & Schuster, 2010).

187 *"win this one for Ike"*: Richard Nixon's August 8, 1968, speech in Miami, Florida, accepting the Republican nomination for president, Richard Nixon Foundation and Library.

188 *"I want you to know how much you have always meant . . ."*: Milton Eisenhower, *The President Is Calling: A Veteran Advisor for the Presidency Suggests Far-Reaching Changes* (Garden City, NY: Doubleday, 1974).

188 *"I want to go . . ."*: John S. D. Eisenhower, *Strictly Personal* (Garden City, NY: Doubleday, 1974).

190 *"The hero has come home . . ."*: Part seven of

funeral coverage, www.youtube.com/watch?v=
mBzVGqOx94s.

193 *"addresses converged on key points . . .":* David Eisenhower, "A Tale of Two Speeches," *Los Angeles Times*,
January 25, 2011.

— INDEX —

234